*Sugar Creek Gang*

# The Lost Campers

Original title:
**Sugar Creek Gang Goes Camping**

# Paul Hutchens

**MOODY PRESS**
**CHICAGO**

# 1

There was a big flood in Sugar Creek that spring, the worst flood old Sugar Creek ever had, I guess. Do you remember the time we went to see Old Man Paddler at his cabin in the hills? I guess there never was a snowstorm like that one either. It snowed and snowed and kept on snowing nearly all winter. That's the reason why there was such a big flood in Sugar Creek that next spring, when all that snow melted.

It there hadn't been a flood in which Little Jim and I *almost* got drowned, then later on in the summer when the gang was up north on our camping trip maybe Poetry and Dragonfly and I all three would have drowned—Poetry and Dragonfly and Little Jim being some of the names of the boys in our gang. I'll introduce you to them in a minute.

So before I can tell you about the tangled-up adventures we had up north, I'll have to give you a chapter or two on the famous Sugar Creek flood.

You see, all that snow melting into water and running across the fields and down the hills into Sugar Creek made him so angry that after he woke up out of his long winter's sleep, he got out of bed (creek bed) and ran wild all over the country. His fierce old brown water sighed and hissed and boiled and roared and spread out over the cornfields and the swamp and the bayou. The creek was like a savage old octopus reaching out his long brown water-fingers. He caught pigs and cows and logs and barns even. He whirled them all away downstream, turned them over and over and smashed them against rocks and cliffs.

Well, a boy isn't always to blame for all the trouble he gets into. Certainly Little Jim and I weren't to blame for there being so much snow that winter. And we couldn't help it that it rained so hard and so much in the spring and caused the flood that was actually the worst flood in the history of Sugar Creek. Although maybe I shouldn't have put Little Jim into a big washtub and towed him out through the shallow water to his dad's hog house which was standing in water about two feet deep. But Little Jim's kitten was up on the top of the hog house meowing like everything. And it looked like the water might get higher and higher. Maybe the kitten, which was a very cute blue and white one with an all-white face and a half-white tail, would be drowned, we thought. So we decided to rescue it before the water crept up any higher. And we had just as well have a lot of fun while we were doing it.

Even a boy knows better than to make a raft and float on it out into a mad creek. And we wouldn't have tried to do such a silly thing, but what we did do turned out to be almost as dangerous. You see, Little Jim's dad's hog house was a low, flat-roofed new hog house. It was standing in very quiet water which had backed up from the bayou into their barn yard. It didn't look a bit dangerous to do what we decided to do. In fact, it wasn't when we started to go out to where the kitten was. And it wouldn't have been at all, if the dike away up along Sugar Creek hadn't broken a wall of water about three feet high. It came rushing upon us and carried us away.

But that's getting ahead of the story. Let me introduce the gang first, in case you've never heard about us. There were just six of us up until the time Tom Till joined. And when he joined that made the number seven, which is a perfect number.

First and best in our gang is Little Jim, a pretty little kid with shining blue eyes, and a grand little Christian. For a while he had about all the religion there was in the Sugar Creek Gang, until the rest of us woke up to the fact that to be a Christian didn't mean that you had to be sad and wear a long face and be a girl. And we found out that Jesus Himself was a boy once just our size, and liked boys even better than our parents do.

Then there was Big Jim, our leader, who had a baby-sized mustache that looked like the little yellow fuzz that grows on a baby pigeon, and who was the best fighter in the country, and who'd licked the stuffin's out of Tom Till's big brother Bob. Did I tell you the Till boys' dad was an atheist? That was why Tom and Bob didn't know anything about the

6

Bible and were as mean as an angry old setting hen when you try to break up her nest.

Big Jim and Little Jim weren't brothers. They were just friends, liking each other maybe better than any of us liked the rest of us, unless it was the way I liked Poetry, which is the name of the barrel-shaped member of our gang. Poetry knows 101 poems by heart and is always quoting one. And he has a mind that is like a detective's. Poetry had a squawky voice like a young rooster learning to crow. And he growled half bass and half soprano when he tried to sing in church.

Then there was Circus, our acrobat, who turned handsprings and somersaults and liked to climb trees better than a healthy boy likes to eat strawberries. Circus's dad had been a drunkard, you know, but had had something happen to him which the pastor of our church called being "born again." After that he was the grandest man a boy could ever have for a father, except of course my dad, who must have been the best man in the world or my mom wouldn't have picked him out to marry him. Boy oh boy! You ought to meet my kinda brownish-gray-haired mom and my grand little baby sister Charlotte Ann. Mom isn't exactly pretty like Little Jim's mom, but she's got the nicest face I ever saw. And even when she isn't saying a word to me, I can kinda feel her face saying the nicest things to me and Dad and Charlotte Ann, kinda like wireless telegraphy or something.

Let me see—where was I? Oh, yes. I was telling you about the gang. Dragonfly's the only one I haven't mentioned in this story. He's the popeyed one of the gang. He has eyes that always make me think of a walleyed pike, and especially of a dragonfly, which has two great big eyes that are almost as large as its head, which of course Dragonfly's aren't, but they're big anyway. And his nose doesn't point straight out like a boy's nose ought to, but turns out right at the end. But after you've played with him a few times and know what a grand little guy he is, you forget all about him being as homely as a mud fence. And you like him a lot.

Well, that's us: Big Jim and Little Jim, and Poetry and Circus and Dragonfly and red-haired me, Bill Collins. Maybe I ought to tell you that I have a fiery temper that sometimes goes off just like a firecracker, and is always getting me into trouble.

And now, here goes the story of the flood that was the worst flood in the history of Sugar Creek. Even Old Man Paddler, the kind, white-whiskered old man who lives up in the hills and was one of the pioneers of the Sugar Creek territory, can't remember any flood that was worse. And that reminds me. That old man knows so many important things and he can tell some of the most exciting tales of the Sugar Creek of long ago. Maybe some day, if I can, I'll put a bug in his ear and see if I can't coax him into writing about the terrible blizzard of 1880. And of old Tom, a trapper whom the Indians got jealous of because he caught so many more beavers than they did, and shot him through the heart with an arrow one morning while he was setting his traps. Old Man Paddler has told us boys that story many a time, so that we know it almost by heart.

Well, after we'd saved the old man's life that cold, snowy day, which I told you about in my book *Winter Rescue*, and after my dad and Circus's dad and a lot of other men had waded through the storm up into the hills to get us, and after we finally got home safely the next day, it began to snow and snow and all the roads were blocked. We had to actually dig a tunnel through the big drift next to our barn before we could get in.

After a while though, a nice long while in which Charlotte Ann kept on growing and learning to say "Daddy" and to sit up without being propped with a pillow, spring began to come. First, here'd be a nice warm day, then a cold one, then rain and more rain, and a warm day. And there began to be a lot of slushy snow everywhere. Then one day in late March, old Sugar Creek started to wake up from his long winter's nap. About a week before the actual flood, when Sugar Creek was still frozen, our gang was standing on the big bridge that goes across the deepest and widest part, looking down at the dirty, snow-covered, slushy-looking ice. All of a sudden we heard a deep rumbling roar that started right under the bridge and thundered all the way up the creek toward the spring, sounding like a big angry thunderclap with a long, noisy tail dragging itself across the sky.

Little Jim cried out like someone had hurt him, "What *is* that?" He looked like he was afraid, which he does sometimes, and Big Jim said, "*That?* That's the ice cracking. It's breaking up. In a few days maybe it'll all break and crack up into a million pieces and go growling downstream. And when it does, boy, oh boy! It'll be something to look at! See those big ugly scars on that old elm tree over there? Away up high almost to the first limb? That's where the ice crashed against it last year. See where the paint is knocked off the bridge abutment down there? The ice was clear up there last year."

*Crash! Roar-r-r-zzzz!*

The ice was breaking up all right, 'cause it was a hot day. All the snow was melting too. We stayed there watching Sugar Creek's frozen old face. I thought about all the nice fish that were down under there. I was wondering if maybe the radio report was right, that it was going to rain for a week beginning that very night, and what'd happen to the little fishies who got lost from their parents and in the swift current were whirled away downstream to some other part of the country.

Well, the radio was right. It began to rain that night, and it kept right on. The ice melted and broke and began to float downstream. It gathered itself into great big chunks of different sizes and shapes and looked like a million great big giant-sized ice cubes out of somebody's refrigerator. Only they acted like they were alive, with the old brown water of Sugar Creek pushing them from beneath. It squeezed its way out through the cracks between pieces and ran over the top, churning and boiling and grinding and cracking and roaring and sizzling and fussing like an old setting hen. I tell you it was a grand sight to see and grand to listen to. We had the feeling all the time that something was going to happen.

And something did happen. Not that day, but pretty soon after that, on a Saturday. I had gone over to Little Jim's house on an errand for Mom, although she and I had just made up an errand so I'd have a good excuse to go over there. You see Little Jim's pet bear had had to be sold to the zoo because it was getting too big to be a pet and was very cross and might get angry some day and hurt somebody. Little Jim's parents had bought a little blue-and-white kitten for him so he wouldn't be so lonesome. As I told you, the kitten's face was all white, and it had a half-white tail, making it about the prettiest kitten I ever saw.

I had on my hip-high rubber boots when I came sloshing into Little Jim's back yard about two o'clock that afternoon. He was finishing practicing his piano lesson, which was a hard piece by somebody named Liszt. The sun was shining down very hot for a spring day. I could hear Sugar Creek sighing about a fourth of a mile down the road. I wished we could go down there and watch the flood, but our parents wouldn't let us stand on the bridge anymore, 'cause it wasn't safe. Some of the bridges farther up the creek had actually been washed out.

The water had filled up the old swamp and the bayou that was on Little Jim's dad's farm. It had backed clear up into their barnyard, making their straw stack look like a big brownish-yellow island in a dirty brown lake.

Little Jim finished his piano lesson and came out to where I was. "Hi, Little Jim," I said, and he said, "Hi, Bill." He still had a sad expression on his face, 'cause he didn't have any baby bear to play with.

"I came over to get some soda," I said. "How's the new kitten today? Where is he? I want to see him. Boy, it surely is a pretty day. Wish we could go down and watch the flood."

He grinned at all the different things I had said. And he sighed and mumbled, "I'd rather have my bear back."

"You could have a bare back if you tore your shirt on a barbed wire," I said, trying to be funny, and not being. Just then I saw his little blue-and-white cat out in their barnyard up on top of a flat-roofed hog house, about four feet high. It was a brand new hog house and had a board floor, Little Jim told me. He knew 'cause his dad and he had built it themselves. They hadn't even set it up on its foundation yet.

Well, that little kitten looked so lonesome up there. How it got up there we didn't know, unless it had been out there

10

trying to catch a mouse, and the water had crept up on it unaware. Anyway, there it was. It was meowing like everything and looked like a boy feels when he's lost.

Well, it looked like a rescue job for lifeguards, which all of a sudden Little Jim and I decided we were.

"Let's go out and get him," I said. There really wasn't any danger, for the water wasn't moving. It had, as I just told you, backed up from the bayou and was just standing there making a big dirty lake in their barnyard.

"We ought to have a boat," I said, looking around for something that might be good to ride on.

It was Little Jim's idea, not mine, to get his mom's washtub. It wouldn't be big enough for two of us, but it would hold Little Jim. And I had on boots anyway and could pull him. Then when we got there, we could put the kitten in the tub too. I could pull them both back to shore, the "shore" being the side of a little hill right close to the barn.

It didn't take us a jiffy to get the tub and to get Little Jim squatted down right in the middle of it, with me on the other end of a long rope pulling him out to the hog house.

*Sqwash, sqwash, slop, splash* went my big rubber boots. Little Jim floated along behind me, grinning and holding onto the sides of the tub with both hands, and with his teeth shut tight, trying not to act scared.

"Where's your dad?" I asked when we were about halfway out to the kitten, which was meowing even worse than before.

"He and Big Jim's daddy are up at the other end of the bayou piling up sacks of sand," Little Jim said. "So the water won't break over and flood our cornfield. 'Cause if it does it'll wash out all the wheat Dad sowed between the rows last fall."

Well, we didn't know very much about floods, except that when we were little we'd heard about one on the Ohio River. But anyway we were having a lot of fun, so we went on out through the muddy water to the hog house. Pretty soon we were there. Little Jim and I climbed up on top of it and sat there in the sun pretending we were on an enchanted island and were pirates. Then we were shipwrecked sailors.

11

Pretty soon we put the cute little fuzzy kitten in the tub and pushed it out into the water—the tub, I mean—with the kitten in it. Kitty didn't seem to mind that, so we left him there while we told stories we'd read in books and talked about our camping trip up north, and how much fun we'd have, and a lot of things. I tied the end of the rope around my leg so Kitty wouldn't drift away.

And all the time *time* was passing. The snow up in the hills was still melting, and all the little rivers and branches that ran into Sugar Creek kept on emptying themselves. And all the time the men were up there at the head of the bayou emptying big sacks of sand on the levee that protected Little Jim's dad's field from the flood.

Then just like time does when a boy is having a lot of fun, two whole hours went past. All of a sudden Little Jim said, "Look, Bill! The water's getting higher! It's almost—*look out!*" And Little Jim began to scream, "We're *moving!* We're—" Little Jim turned white as a piece of typewriter paper. He grabbed hold of me so tight his nails dug into my arm.

I believed it and didn't believe it both at the same time. I looked down at the water which was certainly a lot higher up than it had been, and the back side of the hog house was sliding down deeper. I knew in a jiffy what had happened. That back end was set right at the edge of a little hill. The water had crept up and washed the dirt away from underneath it. Quick as a flash I knew we were in for it. I looked toward the river and the bayou, and there was a great big log swirling down toward us. The black, swirling, muddy water was carrying cornstalks and tree branches and pieces of wood and all kinds of debris. And the great big log was headed right straight toward us.

*Straight* toward us, faster and faster! It looked like all of Sugar Creek was running all over the cornfield below us and that it had picked up all the woodpiles in the country and was carrying them away.

Little Jim held onto me and I held onto him. We both held onto the roof of the hog house, knowing that if the hog house slid down the hill even a little farther, it'd turn over. Or it would slide right out into current, and we'd be carried away.

I tell you I was scared, *so* scared that I was numb all over and I couldn't think straight. Then with a terrible grinding roar the big log crashed into the side of our hog house. And that was the only thing that was needed to break it loose and start it to moving. In a jiffy there we were, floating away, twisting around and around but *not turning over!* And we were being carried down toward the big bridge where Sugar Creek was the maddest of all.

"We—we're *g-gone!*" Little Jim said, his teeth chattering.

And then that little fellow, because he, as I told you, was a wonderful Christian, said, "It's better for us to d-drown than it would be for Little Tom Till, or Big B-Bob, 'cause th-they're not saved."

Imagine that! That little fellow knew that if we'd had to drown right there we would have gone straight to heaven! And that's a lot more than a lot of the smartest people in the world know.

# 2

I tell you, it's a funny feeling, riding on the top of a hog house in flood waters. I guess we weren't moving nearly as fast as we thought we were. But we were moving around in little circles, doing whatever the water wanted us to. Say, if we hadn't been so scared it would have been funny. Coming right along behind us was Little Jim's mom's big washtub, with that little white-faced, blue-and-white kitten sitting in it and looking scared even worse than we felt. Well, I'd heard of boys tying tin cans and things to a cat's tail. But I'd never heard of a washtub with a cat in it being tied to a boy's *leg*.

For some reason it didn't seem very funny, especially when I saw Little Jim's face. I thought, "What if we *do* drown! What if we never see our parents again or any of the gang!"

All the time we were drifting out across the field, getting nearer and nearer to the main part of Sugar Creek where he was madder than a nestful of bumblebees. We weren't drifting straight toward the bridge though. We were moving toward the road, which was up on a high embankment. It looked like we would bump into it first and then follow the current along the edge until it got to the bridge. There, unless something stopped us, the fierce old brown current would grab us and whirl us under the bridge quicker than a flash. And we'd come out on the other side, right in the worst part of the creek and go lickety-sizzle straight toward the big island down below the bridge, where there were some tall trees. Maybe we'd bump into one of them and be stopped and could catch hold of a branch and climb up onto the tree.

"Look!" Little Jim cried. "There's somebody running down the road!"

Sure enough there was. It was Circus, our acrobat. He was running and yelling and waving his arms and trying to get to the place where we were going to hit the bank before we did.

I guess a million thoughts started wrestling around in my head. I couldn't think straight.

And then I saw a telephone pole at the foot of the embankment. I knew what Circus was hollering about. In a jiffy there he was out in the water swimming toward that telephone pole. It was a race between him and us. He got there first, and wrapped his legs around the pole just like he does a tree when he's climbing one. And just that second we went racing past, with the cat in the tub swishing along behind us.

Say, you should have seen Circus's right foot shoot out. It was like an octopus's tentacle grabbing for a man. Quicker'n a flash he'd wrapped it around the rope that was fastened to the tub on one end and to my leg on the other. Before I knew it, I was being jerked loose from the roof of the hog house and from Little Jim and was out in the water. I knew that with Circus holding onto the rope with his foot, if I could get to the telephone pole, I'd be saved. But it all happened so suddenly that before I knew it I had gone under. I came up sputtering and trying to swim. Just as I caught hold of the rope with one hand, I looked back. There was Little Jim lying down on his stomach on the flat roof of the hog house, drifting swiftly toward the bridge and toward the maddest part of old Sugar Creek. I could see his face, still as white as a piece of typewriter paper. He waved an awkward right arm toward us, and yelled in a trembly voice, "GOOD-BYE!" Then he turned around and grabbed hold of the roof with both hands and was whirled away.

I tell you it didn't feel very good to know that I was being rescued and that my best friend might not be. All I could see for a minute, while I was pulling myself by the rope toward the telephone pole, was Little Jim's sad face. And there kept ringing in my ears the words he'd said a little while before that, "It's better for us to d-drown than it would be for Little Tom Till or Big B-bob, 'cause they're not saved!" And I made up my mind right that minute that it was the silliest thing in the world for anybody in the world not to repent of his sins and let Jesus save him. You could never tell what minute something might go wrong and you'd have to die. It's crazy not to be ready. It's the most ridiculous thing in the world!

Even while I was thinking that, and Circus and I were working our way back to the steep bank that leads up to the road, saving the kitten at the same time, I kept wondering if it was too late to help Little Jim. Maybe, I thought, if we could get up to the road and make a dash for the bridge, we could get there in time to reach down and catch Little Jim by the arms and pull him up. The water was pretty high there and if he would stand up, we could reach him easily.

Quicker'n it takes to tell, we were up the bank and running *sqwash, sqwash, kerslosh* down the road in our wet clothes toward the bridge. I was feeling like a boy does in a dream when some wild animal is after him and he can't run fast enough to get away from him. Pretty soon he wakes up and finds out it isn't so. And after he gets over being scared, he is happy again. Only I knew that this wasn't any dream and that I'd have given anything in the world, *anything*, to save Little Jim's life.

Say, it's a good thing Circus's parents were poor. If they hadn't been, Circus would probably have been wearing boots like the rest of the kids in the neighborhood, and he couldn't have run so fast. You should have seen him run! Lickety-sizzle, like a flash of lightning he went down that road leaving me far behind. His feet threw sand and gravel behind him like a horse's feet do when it's galloping.

Panting, gasping, half crying, crazy old tears getting into my eyes, I stumbled on after Circus, not having sense enough to take off my boots so I could run faster. I couldn't help but think of a football game, with the quarterback carrying the ball through a whole tangled up mess of players toward the goal. Only Circus wasn't carrying any old pigskin football full of air but something a million times better. He was carrying the grandest heart a guy ever had, that was full of honest-to-goodness love for Little Jim. I'll bet if the angels that the Bible says are looking after little children were watching Circus streaking down the road to save Little Jim's life, they felt proud of him and felt like screaming for him to hurry up. Only I don't suppose angels ever scream. You know the Bible says in one place, where it's talking about little children, "Their angels do always behold the face of my Father which is in heaven." Jesus said that Himself, and He ought to know. He was in heaven before He came down to earth to be our Saviour. He'd seen maybe a million angels up there.

Just that minute I stumbled over a rock in the road, and went sprawling. When I got up and started toward the bridge again, I heard somebody yelling for me to hurry. I did, not even feeling the bruised place on my right hand where the skin was all scratched off the knuckles of two fingers, from the gravel where I'd fallen.

In another jiffy I was there. But I couldn't see anybody, not even Circus, and away out in the swiftest part of the creek, heaving and whirling, was the hog house and *nobody was on it!*

"*Hurry up! QUICK! BILL!*" I heard Circus yelling, from down below somewhere. And I tell you I hurried, looking all the time, and yet afraid to look below for fear I'd see both Little Jim and Circus down there in the water. As quick as my old water-logged boots would let me, I was there where I'd heard Circus's voice, and would you believe it? There with his legs wrapped around one of the steel beams which stretch from one support of the bridge to another, was Circus. He was hanging head down, with his arms around Little Jim, holding onto him for dear life. Little Jim was holding onto him, and swaying back and forth with his feet almost touching the water, which was all foam-covered and full of cornstalks and slabs of ice. And even while I looked out of the corner of my eye I saw the new hog house downstream bump into a tree and whirl around and turn over on its side.

In less than a tenth of a jiffy I was helping Little Jim climb up Circus's body to the bridge floor, where he was safe. Then I started to help Circus, whose face was very red from hanging down like that, and his legs were trembling, like they couldn't have held on another minute. I braced my feet against the iron girders. And with Little Jim helping a little, but not much cause he was so weak from being so scared,

17

I gave Circus just enough of a pull to help him up to safety too. Say, the very minute he knew he was safe, he just flopped onto the floor of the bridge like an athlete does after he's run in a terrible race. He gasped and panted and his breast heaved up and down something terrible.

But Little Jim was safe, and so was I. And good old Circus was safe too. We were all trembling, and pretty weak, but very happy. I thought I heard Circus say something under his breath about "Lifted me," or something like that. "What'd you say, Circus?" I asked, and he said, "Nothing." But after a while when we were on the way back to Little Jim's house, I heard Circus singing. You know, he had a very beautiful voice for a boy. Little Jim's mom had been giving him voice lessons free, and he liked to sing church hymns very much. He even sang in church sometimes, when they wanted him to. And say, what do you suppose Circus was singing? I wouldn't let him know I noticed it or he might have stopped. A boy nearly always starts to feel bashful when he knows somebody is listening to him. But this is the chorus of the song:

> Love lifted me, love lifted me,
> When nothing else could help,
>   Love lifted me;
> Love lifted me, love lifted me,
> When nothing else could help,
>   Love lifted me.

So away we went. I with my high rubber boots went *splash, swish, kerslosh* through the puddles in the road. Circus, even though his shoes and rubbers were very wet, dodged all the big puddles because his mother had taught him not to walk in mud puddles. Little Jim was still dry. He hadn't even gotten his feet wet. That little fellow could hardly wait until we got back to where his kitten was. And it was still there, sitting down beside the washtub, looking lonesome.

You should have seen Little Jim scoop up that little white-faced kitty and hug it. Circus and I carried the wash-

18

tub between us on the way to Little Jim's house. Pretty soon Little Jim decided to let the kitten ride in it. He walked happily along behind us, looking up at Circus like he thought he was the most wonderful person in the world for saving his life, which I guess he was. It didn't make any different that Circus's parents were poor, and that he couldn't afford a haircut as often as the rest of the gang, and that sometimes his mother had to patch even the patches on his overalls.

Circus was all right on the inside, which is more important than being rich and at the same time being mean or stingy or keeping your heart's door jammed tight shut against the most important Person in the whole universe.

Well, that's the most interesting part of the flood. I'll get busy now and tell you about our camping trip up north, which we took in a trailer that Old Man Paddler bought for his nephew to live in and to give us a vacation in. It was when our parents heard about Little Jim's and my crazy boat ride that afternoon that they decided we couldn't go out in real boats when we were up north, unless we wore what is called life preservers.

And it's a good thing we did, 'cause—

But I'll tell you about that when I get to it, and about a little sad-faced Indian boy whose name was Snow-in-the-Face, and the cream-colored railroad coach Poetry and I discovered away out in the deep woods up there, and a lot of other exciting things.

# 3

When old Sugar Creek calmed down after having lost his temper so terribly, his face was as kind and gentle as a little lamb's face. He had left some of his water standing in little lakes on nearly all our farms. And there were fish in them, which we caught, not with pole and line, but by wading around in the little lakes with our overalls rolled up, until the water got so muddy and thick like gravy that the fish had to stick their noses up for air; and then all we had to do was to walk over and cup our hands under them, one at a time, and pull them out, holding on tight so they wouldn't get away.

Pretty soon it was summer and getting hotter all the time. It kept getting closer and closer to the fifth of July, which was the date on which we were supposed to leave for northern Minnesota on our camping trip. We spent the Fourth of July without shooting off any firecrackers, 'cause one of the boys in our town had burned his hand so badly the year before and that had made all our parents extra cautious. They wouldn't let us have firecrackers. But we didn't much care, 'cause nobody else was doing it.

There was plenty of excitement at our house the Fourth to satisfy me anyway, getting things ready. All the gang had agreed to meet at the spring at two o'clock, to talk things over, and maybe to have a last swim in Sugar Creek. Old Man Paddler's nephew, Barry Boyland, had come from California with the new house-car, or trailer, whichever you want to call it. He had parked it under a big oak tree right close to the spring. He had been living there himself for about a week. There was something especially nice about Mr. Boyland which we all liked.

Barry had been a Boy Scout once, still was one, I guess, and he knew all things a First Class Scout has to know to be one.

Nearly all the gang had already taken their camping equipment down to the trailer. It was planned that we would leave early the next morning. I still had to take my overnight kit down and pack it in with the rest of my luggage, the overnight kit being a long rectangular piece of waterproof material with pockets for a toothbrush, soap, comb, military brush, small mirror and washcloth. When everything was all in it, you rolled it up into a little package. I hadn't wanted to take the washcloth, but Mom said I had to. Dad had said sarcastically, "If you use it a few times, it'll help the Indians up there to identify you as a human being. But don't use it too often or you might catch cold, your face not being used to being exposed to the weather."

Mom had chuckled under her breath at that. Even Charlotte Ann had smiled and bobbed her little head like she thought it was funny, which I didn't.

Pretty soon it was noon at our house on the Fourth. It was a terribly hot day again, making me glad we were going up north to where it would be nice and cool. Mom and Dad and Charlotte Ann and I were sitting around our kitchen table, where we nearly always ate at noon except when we had company. I was finishing my piece of blackberry pie which Mom had baked especially for me, 'cause it was my favorite pie. It was the last piece of Mom's pie I'd get for two whole weeks.

I was all a-tingle inside, thinking about tomorrow, feeling very happy, yet kinda sad, too. I looked across the table at Charlotte Ann, my little twelve-month-old baby sister. I saw her kinda leaning over in her highchair like a willow tree does down along Sugar Creek, leaning over the water, 'cause she was sleepy. Her pretty blue eyes were half shut. Her little round head with its tangle of black curls was nodding like a baby's head does. I felt kinda strange in my heart, like I was in a big vise that was being squeezed shut on me. She's a great little sister, I thought. In fact, she's *wonderful*.

What makes a boy feel that way toward his sister, anyway?

Then I took another bite of pie, using the best table manners I could think of, so my parents would have something pleasant to remember me by while I was away. I looked at Mom who was chewing her pie, and at some new gray hair that was mixed with the brown and which I had never noticed before. Then I looked at Dad who was sitting at the head of the table with his sleeves rolled up. The muscles of his big, brown arms were moving like big ropes that were alive, looking kinda like there was a nest of little snakes inside his arm, and they kept moving all the time and making the brown skin bulge out in different places.

They're grand parents, I though, and I'll bet they'll miss me while I'm away. And all of a sudden I wasn't hungry.

"May I be excused?" I asked as courteously as I could. I'd been reading a book on courtesy that week which my parents had bought for me and which all boys ought to read. The book had made me decide that if I ever wanted to be anybody important in the world, I'd have to have good manners, even when I was at home.

"Excused?" Mom said with a question mark on the end of her voice. "Why, you haven't finished your pie, Bill! I baked it especially for you."

I looked down at my plate and could hardly believe my eyes. I had actually left some of my pie. That goes to show that even blackberry pie isn't the most important thing in the world to a boy who likes his folks. I finished the pie, excused myself again, reminding Mom to be sure to call me as soon as the dishes were ready to be wiped. I went outdoors and down to the barn to say "Good-bye" to the horses and cows and pigs and chickens, and especially to our old black-and-white mother cat whom we called Mixy and who had a whole nestful of brand new black and white and brown and yellow kittens, with the different colors all mixed up.

Old Mol and Jim, Dad's favorite plow horses, were standing quietly in a big box stall, facing each other. Old Jim's nose was kinda pushing up against Mol's neck right where it was fastened onto her head—like my parents stand sometimes when they're looking down at Charlotte Ann in her little bassinet.

Just as I was stooping down to pet old Mixy and to tell her not to feel so bad because I was going away, and not to worry, I heard a squawky voice behind me say, "Hi there, Bill Collins!" It was Poetry who had come puffing into the barn without my knowing he was there.

22

I jumped like I was shot, turned around partway, and said, "Hi there, yourself! Why don't you tell a guy when you're coming! You almost made me jump out of my shoes!" I looked down at my shoes, and I didn't have them on.

"Sorry," Poetry said, meaning he wasn't. "What you looking at so sober-faced?" He came over to where I was and stood looking down into the corner with me at Mixy and her big family of awkward little kittens. All of them had their eyes still shut 'cause they weren't old enough yet to have them open, which baby kittens aren't until they're two weeks old. All of them were eating their dinner in the way baby kittens do. That is, some of them were, and the others were wriggling and nosing around and getting in each other's way and stumbling over each other and falling down, which didn't hurt them 'cause they were so little they didn't have far to fall, which is why it doesn't hurt a boy to fall down nearly so bad as it does a grown-up person.

Old Mixy was looking happy. Her black-and-white tail was waving a little on the end very cheerfully as if she were trying to say, "You aren't the only one to have a nice family. Look at mine!"

Seeing the kittens reminded Poetry of a poem which he started to quote, which goes:

Six little pigs in the straw with their mother;
    Bright eyes, curly tails, tumbling on each other;
Bring them apples from the orchard trees,
    And hear those piggies say, "Please, please, please."

Poetry even sang it, 'cause it was in our music book at school. His voice was so squawky that Mixy actually meowed for him to shut up, or he'd wake up her babies, which were already awake without having their eyes open. Anyway she meowed. He stopped singing, maybe because I pulled his hat down over his eyes with a jerk and told him to.

From Mixy's house we went out to the edge of our pasture which was on the south side of the barn and where there was a big high strawstack. We climbed up on top of it and slid down several times. But it was too hot to play in the

23

sun, so we went back toward our big walnut tree to the swing to get cooled off. All the time I was kinda half waiting for Mom to call me to help with the dishes, which she didn't.

I had planned on going up into our haymow to sit down on the hay and feel sad awhile 'cause I was going to have to leave home. But Poetry's coming spoiled my mood. We decided to go down to the spring to see the trailer and to meet the gang, he having brought some more of his equipment to take down there anyway, such as his camera and a new flashlight. Each one of us boys was taking along a first-aid kit, which had in it a lot of different things and which every family ought to have in their medicine cabinet, in case anybody gets hurt a little. Ours had waterproof adhesive tape, gauze bandage, cotton, Band-aids, Mercurochrome, a pair of scissors, and different things.

Poetry looked at his watch. "I think the gang'll be there early, so we'd better hurry."

"Just as soon as I get the dishes wiped," I said, wishing I didn't have to help do them, but not saying so. A gentleman doesn't say every unpleasant thing he thinks, the courtesy book says.

When I got back into the house, Mom and Dad had the dishes nearly all done. "Why didn't you call me?" I asked, feeling guilty.

"Surprise," Dad said. His big, blackish-red eyebrows were up and he looked at me like he liked me a lot.

"Oh, there's Poetry!" Mom said, looking over my shoulder at Poetry, who was filling most of the doorway behind me. "Want a piece of blackberry pie?" Mom asked him. "We had too much, and with Bill gone there won't be anybody to eat it."

My parents were like that to all my friends, which is why all the boys in the country liked my parents. Poetry ate his pie. Then he and I went down through the woods to the spring.

Just as we got to the top of the little hill that leads down past the old beech tree to the spring, where the trailer was parked, Barry Boyland started up his big black car and drove away. But seeing us, he stopped and waited till we got there.

24

He was wearing a hat with a Boy Scout insignia embroidered on it and a khaki shirt that was open at the neck and had short sleeves, which let his big, brown muscles show like my dad's. And they were almost as big. His face was so tanned it was almost black, and he had a little scar on his cheek where he'd been shot by the police that time I told you about in my first story, when the police thought he was a bank robber.

Barry Boyland had blue eyes that were as blue as a Fourth of July sky. His hair was as black as a piece of coal, and there was one all-gold tooth right in front, which made him look important.

"Here you are, Bill," he said, handing me the key to the trailer. "I have to run into town for half an hour or so. You boys can pack your luggage in the compartment behind the folding bed. I'll stop at your house on the way back and pick up your tent," he said to Poetry.

Holding the key in my hand, I felt important myself to be trusted like that. None of the rest of the gang were there yet. Poetry and I decided to go inside and wait. He could pack his overnight kit and blanket, which each one of us boys had to take with us.

Just as I was inserting the key in the lock, I heard a sound down at the spring. Looking around quick, I saw a red head peeping from behind the big linden tree, or bee tree, as my dad called it, which in June was covered all over with sweet-smelling, creamy-yellow very small flowers, which bees like better than bears like blackberries, or barefoot boys, as Poetry was always saying. The other name for the tree is white basswood.

Well, I knew that that head of red hair belonged to little Tom Till, whose nose I'd smashed once in a fight, and whose big brother Bob was so mean, and whose father was an atheist, and who had never been to church in his life until I got him started, and who was a grand little guy even if he and I both did have red hair.

I finished unlocking the door and pulled it open. Then without knowing I was going to, I called, "Hey, Tom! Want to see what it looks like inside?" All of a sudden I remembered a promise I'd made to myself one day last

25

winter, that some day if I could I was going to do something very important for little Tom Till.

He came out from behind the tree kinda bashful-like, because he didn't belong to the gang. Pretty soon we were inside the trailer, and I was showing him different things. Say, a trailer is a kitchen and dining room and sitting room and bathroom and bedroom and storeroom all in one big, long room.

"See here?" I said to Tom Till, whose blue eyes were open wide with surprise. I lifted up a linoleum-topped trapdoor on one end of a worktable on the side next to the spring, and hooked it up by a little hook so it would stay up. There underneath was a new, two-burner gas stove, which was connected with a great big steel bottle of compressed gas under one of the seats in the dinette, and which you couldn't see without lifting up the seat. At the other end of the worktable was a sink and a water faucet, only you didn't turn the water on like a faucet in a house but lifted it up and down. It pumped the water out of a big, twenty-five-gallon tank which was under the long seat on the other side of the eating table in the dinette. You couldn't see that either.

"Want a drink?" I asked Tom and gave him one out of the faucet.

"Where do you sleep?" he asked, looking around and not seeing any beds.

"Right here," Poetry said, flopping down on a neat, blue davenport.

"Seven people sleep there?" Tom asked with doubt in his voice.

We laughed and said, "Naw, just two. See?" Poetry jumped up, gave the davenport a quick movement which made it turn a somersault. And there as pretty as you please, was a bed wide enough for two or even three boys. All you had to do was to put blankets and pillows and sheets on it, and it'd be ready.

"Some of us'll sleep here," I said pointing to the dinette. "This table comes out and goes underneath. These cushions lie across it, making a nice bed for two. The rest of the gang will sleep outside in tents which we'll pitch close by when we

26

get up there. We're going to park right beside a big lake where we can go in swimming every morning and every night or any time we want to. When we're hungry we throw in a line and hook and catch all the fish we want to. There are so many fish up there that they get all tangled up in your lines—"

Poetry interrupted me to say, "And sometimes we use red-headed boys for bait, the fish are so big."

All of a sudden Tom Till began to look very sad. But I went on showing him the different conveniences: the icebox, the cupboards for dishes, the heating stove which was in a little cupboard about the size of a small coat cupboard, a big two-door wardrobe, and a lot of storage space at the end. There were sockets for electric light bulbs and a place to attach a radio, with a built-in aerial. You could get the electricity from the car for the lights, if you wanted to.

All the time little Tom looked sadder and sadder. Pretty soon, when I looked around he was gone out the door and down past the spring, running toward home. I saw him raise his fist up to his eyes and dab at something which I guessed were tears. I knew that Tom Till wanted to go camping with us worse than he wanted to do anything else in the world.

"Here!" I said to Poetry, "hold the key till I get back." Like a flash I was off down the path after little Tom Till, calling him to stop, which he wouldn't until we got to the bridge. He turned around the corner quick, darted down a steep hill and went underneath, where he stopped in the shade, panting for breath. When I got down to where he was, he was hanging by his legs from one of the rafters under the bridge, pretending to be doing acrobatic stunts.

Say, I liked him better and better all the time. As soon as I could I told him about a promise I'd made myself last winter. That was that I was going to try to get him to join the Sugar Creek Gang. Then I told him a story Old Man Paddler had told us out of the Bible. All of a sudden he spoke up and said, "I won't go to Sunday school while you're gone. Do they have any Sunday school up north?"

"Sure," I said, "and Indians go to them. Did you ever see an Indian?"

27

Just then I heard his dad calling him. He got a scared look on his face, turned pale, and started to climb back up out from under the bridge. I was scared too. I couldn't think of old hook-nosed John Till without remembering the awful sock he'd given me on my jaw once.

"Good-bye," little Tom called back down to me. Pretty soon I heard his bare feet running lickety-sizzle across the bridge toward home, where he'd probably get a licking for something he hadn't done. His daddy was that kind of a daddy, always giving little Tom a licking before he found out for sure whether he needed it. He was not like my dad at all, who always was careful to decide whether I needed one or not before he gave it to me—and most generally I didn't, not anymore.

Pretty soon Poetry was down there beside me. He had a great big whiskey bottle in his hand which he held up for me to see. "Look!" he said. "I found it in Sugar Creek back there by the spring. There's writing in it."

The bottle was corked up tight. And sure enough there was some paper in it, with writing on it, looking like a boy's handwriting.

Well, it was what we found in the bottle that made us decide something very important. Poetry pulled the cork out, and what do you suppose? There was a letter in it written by little Tom Till, and signed by him, with his address. It said:

> Whoever finds this, please read the little printed tract which tells all about how to be saved and go to heaven. And write to me and tell me if you let Jesus come into your heart.

Tom had signed his name to the letter and put his address right below it. And what do you suppose? The tract was one of those our Sunday school teacher had given us the Sunday before at Sunday school and told us to pass out to somebody. Say, I certainly felt ashamed. I'd left mine in my room all week and forgotten them 'cause I was thinking all the time about our camping trip.

Poetry folded the letter carefully, wrapped the tract

28

around it, pushed it back into the bottle, put the cork in good and tight, and with a very sober face, threw it back into the creek. Then he turned to me and said, "I think Tom Till ought to be invited to go with us on our camping trip."

"So do I," I said. We both jumped up and ran back toward the trailer to wait for Barry and the rest of the gang so we could talk it over with them.

# 4

HOT! HOT! HOT!

*Whew!*

That's the way we all felt that Fourth of July. Then came the fifth, just as hot or hotter. We felt fine and very cheerful 'cause we'd soon be on our way up north. By nine o'clock we were all packed and ready, and were actually started. All of us felt like yelling "Hurrah!" when Barry Boyland's big black automobile, with the beautiful silver-topped house trailer on behind, glided down the road, across Sugar Creek bridge, and headed north to the place where we were to camp for two whole weeks.

"Be a man!" my dad said to me while I was in the house just before leaving. He gave me a half a hug like he always does when he likes me. Then Mom gave me a whole hug and said, "Don't forget you're a Christian, Billy-boy!"

Then Dad came over and we had a big three-cornered hug, which we were always having anyway, especially when I was smaller. While Mom and Dad were hugging me and each other at the same time, I reached down and laid my hand on the top of Charlotte Ann's head, making it a rectangular hug instead of a triangular one, her little head being round and as soft as a rose petal.

"Do you have your New Testament?" Mom asked.

"Yep," I said indifferently. And that was the last thing I said. But that little "yep" was a promise to read my New Testament every day and to act like a Christian.

There were eight of us instead of seven 'cause Little Tom Till got to go too. There wasn't room enough for us to all ride in the big black car. Three of us had to ride in the trailer, which was a lot of fun. We took turns, a different group of three every fifty miles so we all got a chance to ride in it. It was kinda like riding in a train to ride in the trailer. Barry made us promise to sit still 'cause it was dangerous not to. If we got to cutting up inside, it might make the trailer sway, and cause an accident.

I tell you it was great, watching the telephone poles and trees go whizzing past and imagining all the fun that was ahead of us.

Barry drove hard all day. And still we weren't there, although the road wound round and round, with lakes or forest on either side nearly all the time during the late afternoon of that first day. At six o'clock we stopped at a lakeside camp and pitched Poetry's tent and another one which we'd brought along.

After supper, which was hot dogs and buns and fruit, the hot dogs being roasted over a campfire, we all played table tennis in a garage close by. When our suppers had settled, we took a swim in the lake which was only about a hundred feet from camp.

WHEW! Talk about cold water! We'd been used to swimming in Sugar Creek whose water in the summertime was almost hot. But the water of this lake was like ice water at first, until we were used to it. Then it was grand.

The sun was still up, although pretty soon it'd go down. The tall trees were making big long shadows on the clear blue water. The little clouds in the east were kinda purple and cream-colored like my mom's irises back home. Some of the clouds looked like the big inch-high creamy foam on the top of our milk pail when Dad's finished milking and is carrying the milk toward the house with old Mixy cat following along behind or running on ahead or rubbing up against his legs and meowing for him to give her her supper.

Pretty soon it was dark. We all put on our sweaters or coats, whichever we'd brought along. Barry stirred up the campfire. The sparks shot up high. The big yellow flames leaped up like Circus's dad's dogs jumping up and down around a tree when there's a coon up there somewhere.

I guess I never will forget that first night. Each one of us told a story, or rather the same story, which Poetry said was a "hash" story 'cause it had so many different things in it and was all mixed up. Big Jim started it. Then when he got to an interesting place he stopped, and Poetry went on from there. Each one of us made his own story as he told it. By the time the story was finished, it was almost time for us to go to bed.

Then Barry Boyland reached over to the campfire with his long stick. He stirred up the sparks, which looked like stars shooting up. We were all sitting around the fire, half lying down and half sitting up. We were waiting for Barry to give us his special campfire talk, which we were to have every night, that being one of the reasons our parents wanted us to go on our camping trip.

While Barry was talking I looked across the fire to where little Tom Till was sitting. His red hair was combed. His big blue eyes were looking at Barry's brown face, and maybe at the scar in his cheek. I could tell that that little fellow thought Barry was greater even than Abraham Lincoln.

I wished all the boys in the world could have heard what Barry said. It was the story of the prodigal son in the Bible, whose father gave him a lot of money and things. Instead of being sensible and saving his money, the boy took everything and started on a long trip. While he was in a far country, he got into trouble and lived a sinful life, spending all his money, just wasting it, and thinking about himself and being selfish. And all the time his dad was heavy-hearted back home because his boy had run away and hadn't come home.

Then one day the boy got a job feeding hogs. He got sadder and sadder and hungrier and hungrier and lonesomer and lonesomer. He was so hungry that he could actually have eaten some of the big long pods of the carob tree which grew in that country and which were good hog food, but not very good for boys—although Barry said that in time of famine even the people over there in that country used to eat them, making a kind of syrup out of the pulp.

"Boys," Barry said, "the heavenly Father has given all of you a wonderful body, strong and healthy, and a good mind. I hope not one of you will ever waste it by not taking care of it. I hope that you'll never have any habits that'll waste your health, or make your mind dirty, but you will be clean and strong. Keep your thoughts pure like—like—" Barry stopped talking for almost a minute, it seemed, before he finished that sentence. He pushed his stick into the fire again, sending up a shower of sparks that looked like big raindrops going up instead of down. Then he started the sentence all over again and finished it. "Keep your thoughts pure like *Jesus*, who was God's only begotten son. The Father in heaven never had to be ashamed of Him."

Things were quiet around the campfire after that, until Poetry's squawky voice started to sing a new chorus which Sylvia's dad had taught us. Pretty soon we were all singing it together, none of us caring that Poetry's voice squawked or that little Tom Till couldn't carry a tune very well. You could hear Circus's bell-like voice above all of ours, singing a kind of tenor. Sylvia's dad, you know, is our new minister back home who likes boys. Sylvia herself is a girl in the eighth grade in school. Big Jim is always especially polite to her.

The chorus goes like this:

> It's a grand thing to be a Christian,
> It's a grand thing I know. . . .

Well, it was time to go to bed. Tomorrow would be there in a jiffy after we got to sleep, and we'd be off again going still farther north.

Barry and Little Jim and I slept in one tent. Poetry and Dragonfly were in Poetry's tent, and Circus and Big Jim and little Tom Till in the trailer.

I was sleeping in what is called a sleeping bag, which is a waterproof bed made out of khaki drill. It has a soft kapoc-filled mattress. You just crawl into it and zip up the Talon slide fastener on the side, and there you are. There is a head flap that goes over the head like an awning over a grocery store window which keeps the rain or dew off your head if you sleep in it outdoors sometime.

I was asleep in a jiffy. And in another jiffy I was wide awake. The luminous dial on my watch which my parents had given me said it was two o'clock in the morning. Say, what makes a boy sleep so fast anyway? I'd actually slept five whole hours in about half a minute!

For some reason I was wide awake, listening to Barry Boyland's heavy breathing. Maybe it was Little Jim's wiggling around on his cot right next to me that woke me up. Just that minute he mumbled something in his sleep. He

33

seemed to be trying to wake up and couldn't. I leaned over and heard him say, "The flood—the water—it's b-better for us to d-drown than for Tom Till—my kitty—here, Kitty, don't be afraid!"

Then that little fellow whimpered and twisted in his bed like somebody was chasing him and he couldn't run very fast. So I reached over with my kinda rough hand and wriggled it around until I found his little soft one. And all of a sudden he took a great big breath and sighed, and was fast asleep with his hand in mine. And do you know what I thought? It's a kind of secret, and having Little Jim for a friend helps to make me think things like this. But I guess it belongs in this story anyway. I thought that if I was a prodigal son and had run away from home and wasted my life for a while, and then was terribly sorry and went back home to my parents or to—to *God*, if He'd just sorta reach out His great big kind hand and put it on mine, I'd know He had forgiven me. And I'll bet if I was tired, I'd go right to sleep without worrying.

I left my hand on Little Jim's a long time so I wouldn't wake him up when I took it away. Outside, the waves of the lake were washing up against the shore, washing and washing. When I pushed my head out through the tent flap, the sky was as clear as the blue on our American flag. The stars were just as bright, only they twinkled like they were alive. For a minute I was lonesome for my parents. The sky with all the bright stars in it made me think of a great big salt shaker that was shaking down little grains of light instead of salt. Or maybe sand, and the sand was getting mixed up with my eyes, making me shut them. And the waves washing on the shore turned into Barry Boyland's heavy breathing, and then mine. And the next thing I knew it was morning, the tent flap was opened, and Little Jim and Barry were gone. Poetry was standing there over me, dropping little drops of water in my face to make me wake up.

Outside the tent the rest of the gang were hollering and running around, pulling down the other tent, and getting ready to start on the last leg of the trip.

34

Poetry threw open the tent flap very wide and let the sun in on my eyes and said:

> A birdie with a yellow bill
> Hopped upon a window sill,
> Cocked his pretty eye and said,
> "Ain't you 'shamed, you sleepy head!"

Which I wasn't, but I zipped down my zipper, rolled out of my sleeping bag, and started off the day with a flying tackle on Poetry's stovepipe-shaped legs.

# 5

I don't know where I got the idea that the Indians up north would be wearing war bonnets on their heads, or have long black hair with all colors of feathers stuck in them. Most of the ones we saw dressed just like us. The boys and girls went around the streets with kinda sad faces which were brown instead of red. And the men and women looked just like brown white people, only the women wore longer skirts that didn't always fit as well as Little Jim's mom's clothes.

We came driving into Pass Lake, Minnesota—which is a town, of course—about two o'clock in the afternoon. Barry went into the post office to see if he had any mail, and to tell the postmaster to send all our mail out to a place called "The Pines." That was the name of the place where we were going to make camp, only the mailman doesn't bring mail out there in an automobile but comes put-putting around the lake in a motor boat.

Well, Pass Lake is a lake as well as a town, and that was the name of the lake we camped on. "The Pines" was the name of the summer resort close by. We parked our trailer on a great big lot that was like a park with a neat little cabin on it. It belonged to a man who lived in Chicago, a great big round man that looked like Santa Claus except for his not having any whiskers, and he was always laughing and likes boys. We named him Santa Claus right away. We called him that all the time we were camped on his lot. And Mrs. Santa Claus! Say, she was a grand little person that looked like Little Jim's mom and had a very special giggle when she laughed.

Santa Claus showed us where to park and helped us pitch the tent. Then he went back to work cutting down small trees on the back of his lot. He'd come up there especially 'cause his doctor in Chicago had wanted him to take more exercise in the open air and see if he could lose ten or twenty pounds of weight which he didn't need.

"See there," I said to Poetry when he and I were driving

in tent stakes for his tent. "If you don't take more exercise and stop eating so much pie, you'll have to chop wood to get thin when you grow up."

Poetry grunted, whacked the tent stake hard with the back of his hatchet, and said, "I'd rather be fat and cheerful like Santa Claus, than thin and grumpy."

You could tell right away that Mrs. Santa Claus, whose first name was Georgia, liked boys. Just that minute she came around to where we were and said, "*Psst!* If you boys would like a piece of pie—"

"Of course," Poetry said politely. He wiped his forehead and licked his chops like a pup does when it sees a piece of steak being held up.

Well, that was the beginning. Different things happened that afternoon. Then we went swimming in water that was still colder than the water in the other lake had been.

That night Santa Claus gave the campfire talk and taught us a new chorus. Next day, Poetry and I had a strange adventure.

It happened like this. The second afternoon, Big Jim and Tom and Barry Boyland took Santa Claus's big white boat with his outboard motor and went fishing for walleyed pike. They left Poetry, Dragonfly, Circus, Little Jim and me to guard the camp, and to fish off the dock if we wanted to, which we didn't 'cause we'd wanted to go fishing in the boat and couldn't. Three was enough to go fishing in one boat, when you're trolling, which is a way to fish that I'll tell you about in another chapter.

The five of us who stayed behind went in swimming. We got cooled off, then we lay around on blankets in Poetry's tent, and slept until Santa Claus came over after having taken his afternoon nap, which the doctor had said he ought to have every day. I could see right away that Santa Claus was beginning to like Circus very much, there not being any children in his family. Some day they might adopt a boy from some orphans' home or somewhere, they said. Anyway, he asked Circus and Dragonfly and Little Jim to drive to town with him in his car to get some minnows, so the rest of us could go fishing when the boat came back, which would be along about five o'clock in the afternoon. That left Poetry and me alone at camp, which had a summer resort about two or three blocks distant on the east and Santa Claus's cabin between us and that. On the other side was forest. And away back up in there somewhere, there was an Indian reservation where Indians lived like real Indians do in the stories we'd read about in books.

Barry hadn't told us we couldn't take a walk if we wanted to. And we certainly wanted to, especially since Poetry had his camera along on the trip, and I had my binoculars. And we needed a chance to use them. So pretty soon when Mrs. Santa Claus strolled over and saw how sad we felt and how much we wanted to take a walk and do a little exploring, she laughed with the very special giggle bubbling up right out of her throat and said, "I think this would be the very nicest place to read my book, so if you boys want to scout around a little, I'll watch camp for you." It was as easy as that.

So, camera and binoculars in hand and a little homemade map of the territory with us, we started out.

We followed the shore for a while. Every now and then we took a look out into the lake and far across to where they were trolling for walleyed pike. When we'd gone about what we thought was a mile, we looked at the map. Then we started off straight north toward where there was supposed to be an Indian reservation, which means a tract of forest land reserved for the Indians to live on.

We walked and walked through dense forest—birch and ash and cottonwood and Balm of Gilead (which is balsam) and spruce.

We were studying trees that summer, making a scrapbook of the leaves of different kinds. So whenever we found a new kind, we wrote it down in a little notebook and picked a leaf, which we put in our hats to take back to camp. Our parents would be glad to know we were interested in things like that.

All of a sudden, Poetry stopped and said, "What time is it?"

I took out my little black-faced watch with its white

numbers. It was almost four o'clock already.

"We ought to be close to the Indian reservation by now," Poetry said, taking out the homemade map. "Let me see. This is south, and this is north. We've been walking straight north for a half hour."

"Have we?" I said. "I thought we turned east back there at the big pine tree."

"East?" Poetry said. "That's where we turned *north*!"

"We did not," I said. And just that minute we heard a sound that sounded like somebody screaming with a quavering voice. We'd heard it a few times before since we'd come up north. Barry told us it was a loon, which is a diving water bird that has very short tail feathers and sounds like a screech owl with a ghost's voice.

Well, if that was a loon, then we knew we were close to a lake. We listened. The sound came from behind us, and the lake couldn't be behind us, 'cause we'd just turned around.

Poetry and I looked at each other with funny eyes. It was time to start back to camp. And we hadn't found any Indian reservation. Just that minute we heard the loon again. It was in just the opposite direction, which it couldn't have been, if it had been where it was before! I stood there all mixed up in my mind, and with Poetry and me looking straight at each other.

We took out the map and looked at it and laughed at ourselves. The map showed there was a wagon trail to to the north of us, and the lake to the south. If we'd go either way, and walk far enough, we'd find either the lake or the wagon trail. After that all we'd have to do would be to go the right direction and we'd come out at the camp.

But which was the right direction?

Neither one of us knew. Poetry didn't have his compass. He'd lost it that snowy day last winter when we'd gone up to see Old Man Paddler—but that's in another story, which you've probably already read.

"If we knew which was was north," I said, "we'd walk to the wagon road. That ought to be closer than trying to find the lake."

"If the road is north, then the lake is south," Poetry said, with his eyebrows down, looking at the map. "Wish that loon'd holler again."

But the loon didn't. And we couldn't tell from the sun, 'cause the sun looked like it was in the north, which it couldn't have been.

I'd never been actually lost in my life, but I began to feel like it. It's a crazy feeling. Any direction you happen to look is either north or south or east or west, if you think it is, which it isn't. That's how you feel when you're lost.

Well, we threw ourselves down on the grass in the sunshine which came down through an opening in the trees overhead.

Poetry had a pucker on his forehead, which meant he was thinking, or maybe just trying to. Suddenly he straightened up. "Give me your watch," he said. I said, "What for?"

He grinned and said, "I want to make a compass out of it. I just remembered something I read once."

He took my watch and laid it down flat on its back in the sun. He looked at it, all the time with that pucker on his forehead.

"Let me see," he said, "one half of what makes what?"

It sounded like some crazy arithmetic problem. And I was never very good in arithmetic. Poetry was the best in his class in school.

All of a sudden Poetry let out a yell. "I've got it! I've got it!"

He looked like he'd got something. "Quick," he said. "Give me a stick about the size of a match. I'll have the directions straight for you in one minute."

Say, I made up my mind that I was going to study arithmetic harder, after I saw what Poetry did. He laid the watch down with its face up and stood the straight little stick up at the outside edge of the hour hand. He turned the watch around until the stick's shadow fell all along the length of the hour hand, which was, of course, pointing straight toward the sun.

"See there!" Poetry exclaimed cheerfully, "straight

south is just halfway between the hour hand and figure twelve on the watch!"

It didn't make sense, but Poetry said it did. He tried to prove it to me with a lot of figures.

"How many hours are there in a day?" he asked.

"Twenty-four, of course," I said. "What's that got to do with which way is south?"

But he ignored my remark, and asked, "How many figures on a watch?"

"Twelve," I said. And he said with a grin, "Right, Bill Collins. Go to the head of the class. And now answer one more question. If it takes the sun twenty-four hours to complete its one-day cycle, how long would it take it to complete a *half* day's?"

I looked dumb and felt dumber. So he said, still with a mischievous grin on his face, "It would take just twelve hours. Now, from exactly twelve o'clock noon to six o'clock in the *afternoon*, the sun would do just one-*fourth* of its day's work. But that's one *half* of a *twelve*-hour day, or one half of the numbers on a watch. So, *two* hours of a *sun's* day, is equal to one hour of a *watch's* day. Therefore," Poetry stopped to make the answer of the problem seem very important, "directly south will be just one half of the distance between the twelve on the watch and the shadow of the stick, which lies straight along the length of the hour hand of the watch. See?" he asked.

Imagine anybody seeing through all that fog! I didn't see. I found out afterward that he was right. I decided then that I had just as well believe the direction he *said* was south *was* south as any other. So we jumped up and started in the direction I thought was north, which he said was south. Every now and then we stopped and looked ahead with my binoculars, hoping to see either the wagon trail or the lake, or anything besides trees and trees and trees, with fallen logs and underbrush and ferns and all kinds of wild flowers and more trees.

Pretty soon Poetry, who had my binoculars, stopped dead still and exclaimed, "Look! There it is! The trailer!

41

What did I tell you! Come on! Let's hurry up!"

It felt good to have that heavy load of being lost off my chest. I started to run too, and then just as quick, we stopped. For what we'd seen wasn't our nice, cream-colored trailer with its silver top. It was a cream-colored, old-fashioned railroad coach! Right out in the middle of the forest!

A railroad coach! Had we lost our minds as well as our sense of direction?

# 6

A railroad coach in the middle of the forest! Well, it couldn't be that, yet it was. We thought at first that there might be a railroad track there, and that we could follow it in the right direction and come to a town, and find out where we were.

But there weren't any tracks, and hadn't been any. We were just as lost as we were before. Poetry and I crept up kinda slow at first until we weren't so afraid. Then we walked up to the steps at one end and knocked on the door.

We knocked again, a half-dozen times. We thought maybe somebody had bought the old coach from a railroad company and had moved it into the forest to live in. On the way up north in the trailer we'd seen some old coaches just like this one, being lived in by people in some of the towns. And some were used for roadside lunchrooms.

Nobody answered our knock. We tried the door to see if it was unlocked, and it was. In a jiffy we were inside, where there were a lot of cobwebs. The old-fashioned cane-backed seats were covered with dust.

The old green blinds at the windows were nearly all pulled down, making it a spooky place and filling our minds with a lot of cobwebbed ideas.

We walked down the length of the coach, feeling all the time like we ought not to be there, 'cause it was somebody else's property. But we kept on exploring it, 'cause we liked mysteries so well. All of a sudden Poetry, who was in the lead, gasped, and stopped. I stopped too, I can tell you. We saw something black between two of the old seats, which were standing back to back.

We could feel our hands trembling on each other's arms. I could feel my feet getting ready to run. "Wh-what is it?" I stammered in a scared whisper to Poetry.

The light wasn't very good, because so many trees outside made so much shade. And the blinds were down. Then Poetry whispered, "Wait." I waited, listening for all I was

43

worth so I could run quick if I had to.

Then Poetry stooped over. Being so fat, the stooping made him grunt, which sounded like an Indian's big ugly grunt. I could feel my hat moving on the top of my red hair, which meant I was really scared.

"It's—well, what in the—" Poetry began, and finished by dragging something out, which made a heavy scraping noise on the floor. We stood looking down at it, feeling foolish, and frightened, and like we were trespassing. "What is it?" I said, making the nerves in my body stop shaking.

"It's an old suitcase," Poetry's squawky voice said.

Well, we'd read in different newspapers about people who had been murdered, and their bodies had been stuffed into trunks or gunnysacks and things. I could imagine most anything being in that big, black suitcase. It certainly was a big one.

We forgot about being lost for a minute, for wanting to solve the mystery. "Let's open it," I said bravely, "and see who's in it."

Poetry's hand was just reaching down to take hold of the handle when I said that. It stopped in mid-air. He looked at me with the strangest expression on his face.

Say, Poetry was brave, even when he was scared. Besides, what was there to be scared of? Just an old, dusty suitcase in an abandoned railroad coach!

I never saw any suitcase open like that one did. It was fastened shut at the bottom rather than at the top—and on the *side* of the bottom at that! But it wasn't locked. So in a jiffy after we'd grunted and pulled a little, it started to open. In another half jiffy it'd have been open if we hadn't been stopped. *Stopped!* We'd heard a noise at the end of the car where we'd entered. Then the old sliding door opened with a rusty squeak that sounded like a screech. And there, standing just inside the doorway, blocking the aisle, was a great big bronze Indian with his war bonnet on and long beads made out of bones hanging around his neck, a big brass bracelet on his arm above the elbow and another around his right wrist. In his hand he held a bow and arrow. There was a big scowl on his face. And standing right beside him was a little Indian boy with black hair hanging down in braids. His face was as quiet as if he had been a statue.

Well, those things happened in books. But they couldn't happen in real life, not to the Sugar Creek Gang or to any members of it! It couldn't be real. The way it was all mixed up, it couldn't be anything but a dream. Imagine! Telling the directions by a stick and a watch! Finding a railroad coach out in the middle of a forest without any railroad tracks. A big black suitcase that opened at the bottom! And an honest-to-goodness Indian with beads and a war bonnet on! In a minute I'd wake up, and I'd be back in my sleeping bag in Poetry's tent.

To make it still more crazy, the little Indian boy behind the big one, didn't *have* a bow and arrow in *his* hand, but a *broom!* An actual broom and dustpan like the kind my mom used back home. And I tell you I wished I was back in Sugar Creek territory, or else that I'd wake up. I didn't care which.

Just when my knees were knocking together and I felt myself sinking down toward one of the seats, the big red Indian smiled. His teeth were beautiful and white. He had long dark eyelashes. When he spoke it was in good English, or I should say, American.

"Good afternoon. What are you doing in my church?"

*Church!* That settled it! It was a dream!

Only it wasn't. "Don't be afraid," the big Indian said. "I won't hurt you. Little Snow-in-the-Face, here, wanted me to dress up in an old-fashioned Indian outfit and pretend we were the Indians of long ago." He smiled again, and said, "Want to see what is on the inside of the suitcase? You're the boys of the Sugar Creek Gang, who are camping over on the other side of the point, aren't you? I know about you. Snow-in-the-Face and I have been following you, thinking maybe you were lost. We were going to help you find your way back to camp." He was using almost perfect language and there wasn't much Indian accent.

"Who-who are you?" Poetry stammered. He was still scared. I was still dreaming, I thought. I kept on *half*-thinking it until a minute later, when the big Indian took off his war bonnet and laid it down on a seat, and said, "Here,

Snow-in-the-Face, let me have that broom. We'll have to get busy if we want to get our church swept and dusted and ready for the meeting tonight."

Little by little we came to our senses. And this is what we found out. The big Indian was telling the truth. It was a church! The members of Santa Claus's church back in Chicago had bought an old railroad coach and had had it moved out into the forest on the Indian reservation to be used as a church, it being almost as cheap to buy a church as to make one. Snow-in-the-Face and his big brother, whose Indian name was Eagle Eye, were Chippewa Indians. Eagle Eye had become a Christian when he was a boy twelve years old. He had been away to school—high school and a real Christian college—where he was studying the Bible and how to be a missionary to his own people. He had just come home for the summer. He was going to have meetings in the old railroad coach. The members of Santa's church in Chicago were going to support him as their own missionary. Say, if every church in the world would support one missionary, the rest of the world would get converted quick, I bet. Poetry figured it up once. He says it's so, and Little Jim wishes it was.

Well, it was like getting out of a whirlwind alive to come out of all that tangled-up mystery without getting hurt. Camp was just on the other side of the point from us, Eagle Eye said. He'd drive us around there after a while in an automobile, if we'd help him clean up his church. The old wagon trail was just *south* of us a little way.

"Like to see the suitcase?" Eagle Eye said. He lifted it and carried it down to the other end of the coach where there was a little platform. He opened it up. And it wasn't a suitcase at all, but a little folding organ, with keys, and pedals and a rack for a hymnbook, and everything.

It didn't take us long to finish the work. Then we drove back to camp in Eagle Eye's kinda old car, which was parked the distance of about two blocks away. We got there just about the same time the fishermen came in with a big string of walleyed pike. I took out my watch to see what time it

46

was. And Poetry who was in a very good humor looked at me and said, "What direction is it?"

"Five minutes after south," I said, grinning, feeling better than I had for a long time. Just that minute Santa and Dragonfly and Circus and Little Jim came driving into camp in Santa's big car. For the first time little Snow-in-the-Face smiled. He climbed out of Eagle Eye's rickety old car and shuffled over to the other one to get a sack of stick candy which Santa had brought for him, and which he must have been expecting, he and Santa being very good friends.

We heard someone calling us from the dock about that time. It was little Tom Till, standing up in the boat, which was in very shallow water, and holding up the biggest string of the biggest fish I'd ever seen in my life, making that little old nine-inch bass which Dragonfly had caught in Sugar Creek last summer seem very small. Very *very* small.

## 7

Not only was there a big string of big fish, but there was one stringer on which there was just one fish that weighed twelve pounds!

Whew! Talk about fish! Say, that great big northern pike had a mouth almost large enough to get a boy's head into it. And it had sharp teeth like a saw's teeth. Its nose was long and ridiculous looking. I couldn't help but wish I'd caught it myself, so I could have my picture taken with it, like Big Jim was having done to him right that minute. It was he who had caught it.

As I told you, Santa had gone to town to get some minnows, which they keep there in a live bait store, so that the rest of the gang could go fishing when the first boatful of fishers came back. So now it was our turn. Only there were still too many of us. It wasn't any fun to try to troll with more than three in a boat at one time. The lines would get in each other's way.

We finally decided to let Barry Boyland rent another boat from the boat livery at the resort, so all the rest of us could go. Santa Claus took Circus and me in his boat. Barry took Dragonfly and Little Jim and Poetry. Little Jim said he wouldn't fish but would just go along for the ride, and he'd holler every time anybody caught a fish, which made Poetry say, "Then we don't want you in *our* boat, 'cause we don't want you to be yelling every minute! Go over and get into Bill's boat, so you can keep nice and quiet!"

I had my dad's light steel pole with a reel and all the latest fishing equipment, although I didn't know how to use it very well. It was fun learning how though. Santa showed me the best way to do it. We were soon out on the lake, put-putting away over the waves. Riding in a big boat on a big lake felt like sitting in Mom's favorite rocking chair at home. Only the boat didn't only rock backward and forward but sidewise and every other direction, whichever way the boat turned. Sometimes it seemed like it was rocking in a half-dozen directions at once.

Well, trolling was great fun. The lake wasn't very rough at all. Even if it had been we wouldn't have been afraid, because we were all wearing our life preservers, which our parents had bought for us, because the flood in Sugar Creek last spring made them cautious. The vests were kinda awkward, but we got used to them, knowing that if a big storm should come up, or if anything did happen, such as a boat turning over, we'd all float in the water, with our heads up. And if the wind would keep on blowing we'd drift to shore somewhere.

I'm sorry to have to say that we caught about five fish on our trip out, although I could hear Little Jim and everybody else in the other boat making an awful noise. Their boat had gone on ahead of us. It was around on the other side of the point, so we could hear them but not see them very well.

On the way back, I kept feeling kinda sad because we had only five walleyed pike, none of which was over fifteen inches long. The others would surely have almost a boatful with all the noise they were making. But when they came in, they had only two or three big rock bass, and Poetry's line was all tangled up and broken. He had lost the hook and leader and a fish that must have weighed twenty pounds, he said.

There was plenty of excitement in that boat though. Everybody was talking at once, telling how big the big fish was that got away. Poetry was still shaking from the excitement of having had the fish on his line and almost but not quite landing it.

Poetry carried his pole and tangled-up line sadly toward camp. The rest of us followed along behind, feeling sorry for him. "I tell you it was *that long!*" Poetry said measuring off about three feet on the pole, "and it weighed twenty pounds!"

"How much?" Big Jim asked, grunting and holding up his own twelve-pound fish and admiring it.

"Twenty!" said Poetry again. "Why, it felt like a great big dog on the other end of the line!"

Then Big Jim laughed, and said, "Ha! If mine had gotten away, I'll bet it would have weighed twenty pounds too. But on the scales it only weighed twelve."

Poetry looked at him disgustedly. Then he walked away and began to untangle his fishing line. I went along with him to help him, and Dragonfly came too to keep us company.

Pretty soon we heard Barry calling for all to come and have our first lesson in cleaning fish. I didn't want to go at first. If there was anything in the world I hated worse than hoeing potatoes or wiping dishes, it was cleaning fish.

Say! It was as easy as eating blackberry pie, the way Barry cleaned those fish. He didn't even scrape the scales off but just laid the fish down one at a time on a flat board on the table. Beginning at the tail with a long sharp knife, he just sliced that fish right up along the center and came out at the gills, and there was a nice piece of fish steak which restaurant menu cards call *fillet of fish.* Then Barry turned over the half of the fish that was left and did the same thing, slicing all the way up, right along the edge of the backbone and coming out just below the gills. Quicker'n nothing there was another great, big, snow-white steak, each one of the steaks still having the skin and scales on one side.

Then Barry picked up the fish's head. All the insides were still fastened to it, and the backbone and the fins and tail. He dropped it into a big paper sack. *He didn't even have to touch the insides!* Which is why I'd never liked to clean fish.

I forgot to say that he had held the fish with his left hand and used the knife with his right. And he had a dry cloth in the left hand to keep the slimy fish from sliding out of his grasp.

Well, there was nothing to do now but to take off the scales and the skin, which was as easy as peeling a banana. All Barry did was to lay the steak down on the flat board with the scales side *down.* Then he caught hold of a tiny piece of the tail end. He slid the sharp-bladed knife back and forth like it was a saw, pressing it down all the time, and in about four seconds, there was a swell piece of all-white steak, white on both sides with no bones in it except the ribs.

It didn't take long to clean them all and to put them on ice in the icebox. Then we had supper, and another campfire meeting, and went to bed again.

It had been an exciting day. But we were so tired that we

slept like eight logs being sawed with noisy saws, which means we snored.

For the next day, Barry had planned what is called a first-aid hike, which real Boy Scouts are always taking. We'd been up here for three days now, and nothing very exciting had happened, that is, no real adventure, except being almost scared to death by an Indian.

Before going to sleep that night, I thought cheerfully of what was going to happen tomorrow. We'd get a chance to see what the north was really like. We'd never had a first-aid hike, although I suppose Big Jim had, 'cause he was a Boy Scout. And of course Barry had.

*Tomorrow!* I was sleeping in Poetry's tent, with Little Jim lying right beside me in his own sleeping bag. He was already breathing away noisily like a boy breathes when he's asleep. Say! It even helps a person to go to sleep, when he's got what is called insomnia, if he just pretends he's asleep and starts to breathing kinda lazy-like and with a noise that sounds like my dad's handsaw cutting through a board.

For just one little minute I stuck my head out of the tent flap to look up at the stars, and at the little grains of light I liked to imagine were sprinkling down. There was a great big yellow moon just pushing its head up out of the lake away out there where the sky and the lake were fastened together. That big moon was the same moon that was just coming up down along Sugar Creek too, I thought, and at the very same minute. I wondered how it could do it. I also thought that maybe about that very minute down in Sugar Creek territory, my great big dad and my very kind-hearted mom might be sitting out on our side porch, holding hands, each one in a chair kinda close to the other one. And maybe Dad would call Mom one of his favorite names for her, and say, "I wonder if our Billy-boy is lonesome for his parents." And Mom would kinda giggle a little and say, "Sure he is. There isn't a boy in the world that likes his parents better than our Bill." Then Mom and Dad would stand up and look at the same moon I was looking. And then they'd go in the house and go to bed.

# 8

It was Poetry's *almost*-and-yet-not-quite catching that big fish that got us into trouble later on, near the last of the first week. He couldn't get over the fact that he'd lost it. He made up his mind that before the camping trip was over he was going back there and catch that fish, if it was the last thing he ever did. He told me about it. And he talked about it every day.

As I said, the very next day after he'd lost it, Barry had planned a first-aid hike. We'd be gone all morning and wouldn't get back in time to get dinner. He said we'd put our fish dinner on to cook right away. That is, we'd put it on at ten o'clock, which was the hour set for the first-aid hike.

We'd been cooking nearly all our meals on the gas stove in the trailer. But today's dinner was to be an Indian dinner, cooked in the ground. I'd never heard of such a thing, but I was willing to do my part. Barry put us all to work—after breakfast and after we'd had a little talk from the Bible by Santa, who came over just in time.

My job to help get the dinner ready was to dig a hole in the ground eighteen inches each way, that is, eighteen inches deep and the same distance in every other direction. I got a shovel from the resort and went to work. Poetry and Little Jim and Circus were sent to gather stones, about a couple of bucketfuls, enough to completely line the hole. The idea looked silly but Barry told us to do it, so do it we did. Poetry set his rocks down with a grunt beside me and said, "Be sure you dig it far enough south."

Pretty soon the hole was finished and lined with rocks, each one pushed up close against the other. Big Jim put in kindling wood, and dry twigs, making a pile about two feet high, putting the sticks in a crisscross style. Then he started a fire. We let it burn for a whole hour, while we did different things around camp, waiting for the wood to all burn up. Barry sent us after basswood leaves and wild grape leaves and leaves from sassafras shrubs. We even got some lettuce leaves which we found in the icebox.

"All right, Bill, bring your shovel," Barry called, which I did. "Now scoop out all the ashes and live coals and pile them here. Circus, get a bucketful of sand quick. Dragonfly, get those old burlap sacks there by the trailer door and soak them in the lake. Bring them here as wet as you can."

It still looked very strange to us, but we obeyed anyway. In a jiffy I had all the coals scooped out, leaving nothing in the hole but hot stones. Barry lined this with the green leaves. And quicker'n anything, he put in about a dozen great big steaks of fish right in the center of the hole. All around the fish he put potatoes, and corn on the cob and carrots.

On the top of that he spread more green leaves and more stones. Then he laid on the soaking-wet burlap sacks, just as Circus came puffing up with a pail of sand from the beach. On top of that Barry made me scoop some more sandy soil, making a little mound.

Well, to me it didn't make sense. It looked like the end of a funeral, with the fish being the corpse. All we needed now was a tombstone and it would all be over. So I said to Poetry, calling him by his real name, which is Leslie Thompson, "Leslie," I said solemnly, "go get your fishing pole, the one you caught the twenty-pound fish with, and set it up for a tombstone," which made him turn red in the face. He said, "Just you wait and see. I'm going to learn *how* to fish. And before we go back to Sugar Creek, I'll catch that big old northern, if it's the last thing I ever do," not knowing that it would come mighty near to *being* the last thing he'd ever do. Why if it hadn't been for—but that's too far ahead of the story. I'll get to that pretty soon, though. First, let me tell you about our first-aid hike.

Well, with the "funeral" over, Barry handed me a white envelope, saying, "You're the guinea pig today." You see, a first-aid hike is one in which some boy of the gang or Scout patrol is given an envelope with instructions in it, telling him what kind of an accident he is to *pretend* he has had. He doesn't know himself, until he opens the envelope, just what is supposed to have happened to him. He walks along ahead of the gang, starting five whole minutes before they do. Then

53

after five minutes, no matter where he is, he stops, opens the envelope, and reads the instructions. Whatever it says, he does. Sometimes he has to pretend he's fallen out of a tree and broken his arm, or leg. Sometimes he has fainted, or fallen into the lake and drowned, not really, of course. The rest of the gang come along, find out what's happened, and administer first aid. It's good sport and good training.

We were just ready to start, when we had a case of real first aid to take care of. Poetry had reached up under his shirt to scratch his side, when he felt something funny there, kinda like he'd run a sliver in. So he jerked back his shirt tail and looked. And there was a little wood tick sticking head-first right into his fat side. In fact, that little tick's head was completely buried, Now, I'd read about wood ticks in a book. And they're dangerous if the head gets left in when you pull them off. You might even get a fever and be sick.

It didn't take long to take care of the tick, though. Big Jim knew exactly what to do, and Barry let him do it. He sent Dragonfly after a match in the trailer. Then he lit the match and let it burn until there was a red hot coal on the end. Then as quick as a flash he touched the hot end of the match to the tail of that little wood-tick, being very careful not to touch Poetry himself. Say! You should have seen that little flat rascal of a wood tick wiggle and squirm and come backing out of Poetry's side. It was like our old Jim horse backing out of his stall, or else like what my dad's car does when he backs it out of the garage and is in a hurry to get to town—although Big Jim did have to use another match to make him back all the way out.

And now for the hike. I took the white envelope and started off down the lake shore, only to be stopped by Poetry who yelled, "Hey, what direction are you going!"

"Keep still!" I yelled back at him. I went on, minding my own business, wondering all the time what was written on the paper in the envelope.

I was supposed to walk along the lake shore, Barry had told me, until I came to where the big point of land starts to go out into the lake. Then I was to keep on following the shore line until I came to a boat belonging to Eagle Eye and his brother little Snow-in-the-Face. There I should stop and read my instructions.

So I started out. It was a grand morning, with the lake looking like a great big silvery-blue mirror with live wrinkles on its face. Already I could see the point of land which jutted out maybe a half mile into the lake, something like a long neck without any head.

That was where Poetry and I had been lost that other day before we knew very much about the territory up there. That explains why we could hear a loon first on one side of us and then the other. There had been two loons. They were hollering to each other across the neck of land, like two boys hollering to each other across a schoolyard.

On the other side of the neck was a sandbar. Nearby were schools and schools of walleyed pike that liked to chase after minnows.

On the other side too, was a big, long shoreline of bulrushes, where, in different places, some big northern pike lay in hiding on the bottom of the lake waiting for a live breakfast or a live dinner or supper to come swimming along. Then they would shoot like torpedoes under the water straight toward that dinner.

If that live dinner happened to have a hook in it with a boy on the other end of the line, the northern pike himself turned into a dinner for a hungry boy.

While I was walking along I thought that I would like to be a fish, living down in the interesting under-water world, with all the strange-looking other fish all around me. I'd go on an exploring trip, down, down, down to the very bottom of the lake. Maybe I'd organize a special gang of fish and have a lot of fun. There'd be a big northern pike and a little northern pike, a fat sunfish and an acrobatic bass, a very walleyed pike, and a red-finned, spotted muskellunge which would be me with my red hair and freckles.

Just that minute I heard a big motor boat go put-putting by on the lake. I knew it was mailtime at camp. In my mind I could see the gang all running down the long deck toward the mailbox at the end to see if there were any letters from home.

Pretty soon I came to the white boat that belonged to

Eagle Eye and his little brother Snow-in-the-Face. There I stopped and tore open the envelope. I read the note inside which was written with a typewriter. "Dear Guinea Pig," it said. "Find south by using your watch. Then walk straight west until you come out on the other side of the point, where you will find a sand-bar willow, growing right at the edge of the water. There you are supposed to drown yourself, only please don't do it.

"Wait in the shade of the willow until you hear us coming. Then slide off into the shallow water and call for help. Play dead until we get to you. After we get there, play dead for five minutes until we've restored your breathing by artificial respiration. We'll let you know when you're alive again."

I finished reading the note, put it back into its envelope, shoved it into my pocket, took out my watch, and picked up a little stick about the size of a match. It was just half-past nine, I noticed, not nearly as late as I thought it was.

I laid the watch down on the palm of my hand. I set up the stick on the outside of the rim of the watch. I turned the watch around until the shadow of the stick fell straight along the hour hand. South, I knew, would be just halfway between the point of the hour hand and the figure 12 on the dial.

Anybody could find west, if he knew which way south was. So I grinned to myself and started west. I walked along, feeling happy, thinking of a lot of cheerful things, glad I was alive and remembering some of the important things Barry or Santa had been telling me in the campfire talks. I was beginning to get hungry too, thinking about the buried dinner under the old wet burlap sacks back at camp.

Yes sir, I tell you it was great to be alive. A rabbit jumped up—a little reddish-brown one—and scooted across in front of me. A crazy loon let out a weird noise from the lake, like some of the soprano women's voices that sing on radios, which I always turn off as soon as they start. I'd much rather hear a loon. It knows when to stop without being turned off, I thought. Another rabbit jumped up just then and started to run, going right straight west, the same direction I was going.

Or was it north? All of a sudden I had a funny feeling. Every direction I looked was the same direction. There were trees and trees and more trees. It was just like it had been that other time when Poetry and I had been lost.

But I didn't worry. I knew how to find directions now myself. I took out my watch, and would you believe it? It was still half-past nine! My watch had stopped running, and had maybe been stopped for a long time! Why, it ought to be almost eleven by now, I thought. And if I could have told the time with my stomach, it would have been way after twelve, I was so hungry.

I stood still, thinking. We must have put the Indian dinner in its grave about ten o'clock. Then Poetry had had to be operated on. Hm! Let me see, I thought. It ought to be about eleven by now.

But that would change the directions all around! It meant that I hadn't been going in the right direction at all. I might miss the willow tree when I got there.

Anyway, I set my watch forward to eleven o'clock, wound it, and found south again. Then I started out in the direction I thought I was supposed to go, feeling funny and wondering, What if I get lost again! Barry had said in his talk last night, "See there, boys? That's why we have to have the Bible, which is God's Word, to show us the right direction to go. Nobody would know right from wrong, or how to live at all, or how to go to heaven, if we didn't have this compass." Then Barry had held up the Bible for us to see. I had reached into my vest pocket, where I always kept my New Testament, and felt proud to think that my parents knew enough to buy me one, and teach me to read it.

I kept on walking though, knowing I was going pretty near right and that sooner or later I'd get across the neck of the forest, which I did. In about three minutes more I heard the washing of waves against a shore. And there was the lake, and the sandbar and the willow, near the water's edge.

I waded out through the soft white sand and lay down in the shade of the little tree, wondering why the shade should be on the south side of the tree at noon when it was supposed to be on the north. Oh well, I thought, I never was very good at *feeling* directions. So I quit worrying about it. It didn't matter how I felt. South was south, and nobody could change it, just like the Bible which says, "Believe on the Lord Jesus Christ and thou *shalt* be saved," and that settles it!

I tell you, we boys liked Barry Boyland. And we thought our parents were the wisest parents in the world to give us that kind of vacation.

Pretty soon the gang would be coming to bring me back to life again so I lay there thinking and imagining what if I *was* dead!

I guess my mom and dad and little Charlotte Ann would be lonesome without me. And I'd be lonesome for them, even in heaven, maybe. First they'd take the little red-haired, freckled-faced body that I used to live in out to the evergreen cemetery behind our church and bury it. And everybody would cry and cry and feel very sad, Mom and Dad most of all. And we wouldn't be able to have any more of our three-cornered hugs—I think maybe I'd miss that most of all.

The gang would miss me too. And Old Man Paddler—I would even get to heaven before *he* did. But I'd tell Jesus the kind old man was coming pretty soon though. Maybe some day up there I'd walk down a quiet sort of lane, with a lot of birds singing in the trees on each side. And there, upon a pretty little hill, would be a kinda oldish-looking cabin, all fixed up for Old Man Paddler to live in when he came. I don't think he'd want to live in a great big swellish house. He'd rather, if it cost anything to make it, have Jesus save the money to help the missionaries preach the gospel to the heathen. Or else help some poor boys get a good chance in life down on the earth.

I might even walk up to the oldish-looking cabin some morning and kinda look after the flowers for him, so that when he got there, everything'd be just like he'd like to have it. Then I'd get a drink at his spring, if I was thirsty. Sylvia's dad says we won't ever get thirsty in heaven. Maybe the Bible means, though, that a boy can always have all the water he wants. Anyway, maybe Jesus Himself would come walking along with the scars still showing in His hands where He'd suffered on the cross for everybody. And He'd

58

smile and kinda lay one of His hands on my head and say, "Thank you, Bill. Whatever you do for others who love me, you do for me." And maybe He'd give me the same kind of a hug my great big dad does.

Well, that's as far as I got to think just then. All of a sudden I felt something cold touch my nose. I opened my eyes quick. And would you believe it? There was a little blackish-green turtle with silly, blinking eyes looking right straight into mine, not more than a few inches away. In fact, I had to look cross-eyed to see him, he was so close.

I knew right away that I wasn't in heaven. I'd seen little turtles like this one before, down along Sugar Creek. They were always swimming and diving around in the water. Sometimes they'd crawl up on the land and travel to different places. Turtles even migrate like birds do, although they don't move in such big companies like birds or grasshoppers. And that reminds me. When Old Man Paddler was a boy, grasshoppers used to be so thick sometimes that when they'd fly or migrate from one part of the country to another, they'd actually hide the sun like a big cloud does. It'd be almost dark on the earth.

Well, sometimes when turtles migrate, or, anyway, shuffle around up on the shore, they *some*times try to cross the road. And they get run over, not having as much sense as a boy who looks both ways before he starts, and waits if he doesn't have time enough to get across first.

Well, this little guy was as surprised as I was. And he didn't seem to like me any better than I did him. He turned around as quick as anything and scrambled away toward the willow tree. He started head-first into a patch of grass there, kinda like a flat wood-tick squirming headfirst into a boy's side, carrying his bony house with him, like turtles do. Ho hum! I'd hate to have to carry a house with me wherever I went, although I suppose if it was a part of me, I wouldn't mind it so much.

Just at that minute I heard the gang coming. I rolled over a couple of times and went *kersplash* into the water. I screamed a wild scream for help, splashed around a little and sank to the bottom. The water was only about eight inches deep. I lay on my back with my face and nose sticking up like a turtle's nose does when it's in the water and just looking around. Only I kept my eyes shut.

I screamed another blood-curdling scream and kept on lying still with my eyes shut.

I could hear footsteps running across the sand, *sqwash, swish, crunchety, crunch-crunch-crunch,* like the noise a boy makes when he is eating dry crackers.

I kept on keeping my eyes shut, and my lips too. I tried hard not to grin, thinking of how cold the water was and of hook-nosed big John Till's big hard fist. That kept me from smiling.

Then for a fraction of a second, I opened my eyes and shut them quick. And would you believe it? I couldn't believe myself at first. It wasn't the gang at all. It was little black-haired, black-eyed Snow-in-the-Face.

# 9

I never saw anything look stranger than little Snow-in-the-Face's face when he was looking down at me, lying there in the water. He was really worried.

He couldn't talk American very well, but only Chippewa, which means that at home, his parents must have talked Indian. But he could grunt and talk jerkily like Indians do in storybooks. He had strawberry stains on his thick lips. I was pleased to see that. It must have meant that there was a patch of wild strawberries around there somewhere, which I could find sometime, when I came back to life. Even Indian boys like wild strawberries, I thought, which shows that they are just people.

Quick as a flash he stooped down. He caught hold of me to try to lift me out of the water. He was only a little smaller than I was, but he was very strong. Of course I couldn't let him pull me out. Any minute the gang might come along, so I groaned and fell back limp.

"What's the matter?" he grunted. "Back hurt?"

"No," I moaned. "I'm all right. *Oooooh!*"

"White boy leg broke?"

I shook my head.

He was down in the sand at the very edge of the water, trying to get his hands under my neck. But I wouldn't let him.

"Where hurt?" he asked anxiously. "I go get Eagle Eye. Take you home."

"No, no!" I groaned. "Leave me here. I-I'm sick!" *There,* I thought. *That'll make him quit trying to pull me out of the water.* For pulling me out of the water was the gang's job, if they ever came. Poor little Indian guy! He was so sorry for me.

"Maybe stomach hurt?" he said. "Too many strawberries?"

That made me hungry. And seeing that little Indian boy

made me still hungrier. It made me think of the Indian dinner that was buried back at camp. I wondered if all we'd have when we dug it up would be a lot of raw fish and potatoes and corn-on-the-cob and carrots. I made a face at the thought.

"You *very* sick," Snow-in-the-Face said. "I get Eagle Eye quick!" He scrambled to his feet, getting sand in my face and eyes at the same time.

"*Stop!*" I yelled. "I'm not sick. I—I'm *dead!* I drowned a few minutes ago!"

He did stop, with the queerest expression on his face. Then he grunted and said, "White boy crazy in the red head!" He started to go again. But just that minute there was a noise up the shore like more boys eating crackers. I looked, and there was the gang coming toward me—Big Jim and Little Jim, and Circus and Poetry and Dragonfly and little Tom Till. And Barry Boyland.

The way Barry gave orders was grand. He made his voice sound very authoritative, like I had really drowned and had to be brought back to life. "Quick!" he commanded. "Poetry, go telephone for Dr. Dragonfly. Circus, you run back to camp for a blanket." Only the blanket was already there. They'd brought it along with them to wrap me in.

Little Snow-in-the-Face piped up and said, "I go get blanket. Not far away." But they wouldn't let him.

The next five minutes there was a lot of pretended excitement. I had found the wrong sand bar and the wrong willow tree. That is why the gang hadn't found me sooner. If they hadn't seen little Snow-in-the-Face, I might have had to wait still longer.

The gang pulled me out of the water. Then they started working on me to give what is called *artificial respiration*. That is what they do with a boy who has quit breathing but whose heart has not stopped beating. And even when the heart *has* stopped beating, they do it sometimes just in case it *really* hasn't. Maybe the boy's soul is still in him, not having gone to heaven yet—if he was a *saved* boy, which means if he had believed on the Lord Jesus as his own personal Saviour.

I tried to imagine how I looked lying there as pale as a ripe tomato, with my hair all mussed up. I could have been called "Dirt-in-the-Face." Thinking that made me start to grin. But I stopped quick by thinking of hook-nosed John Till's big hard fist.

"Start to work quick!" Barry commanded. "Waste no time carrying him anywhere! Save the seconds and you have a better chance of saving his life!" That sounded sensible and is what real Boy Scout leaders teach.

I guess Barry had explained to the gang ahead of time just what to do. He had appointed Poetry and Big Jim to work on me. They flopped me over in the sand, stomach down, with my right arm extending up above my head. They bent my left arm at the elbow. They slipped it under my face, which was turned sideways toward my right arm, letting me have the back of my left hand and the crook of the arm for a pillow. This kept my nose and mouth out of the sand so I could breathe.

Then Big Jim went down on his knees, straddling my right leg, and began to work on me. All of a sudden I felt the palms of his big hands on the small of my back at the bottom of my ribs. It seemed like the whole weight of his body was pushing down on my back, squeezing all the wind out of me and making me grunt. Poetry said, "He's alive, all right," but Big Jim shushed him.

Then Big Jim's hands were off again, and then on again. First he'd press down with all his strength, then he'd straighten up, wait only two seconds, and forward he'd come again, and press down with all his strength. When you do that to a boy or anybody who has drowned, you might start his lungs working again and save his life.

Up, down, up, down. Big Jim was awfully heavy. I wished they'd hurry up and tell me I was alive, so I could rest. I felt sorry for all the people in the world who had the kind of polio that paralyzes what is called the "respiratory muscles," so they can't breathe.

You know, 3 people out of every 100 who do get polio have to be put into what is called an iron lung, which works just about like Big Jim was working on me right that minute. It keeps them alive until maybe their lung muscles get strong enough to do their own work.

Up, down, up, down. I wished Dr. Dragonfly would hurry up and come.

I could hear Big Jim breathing hard behind me, getting tired himself. I opened my eyes. Little Snow-in-the-Face was still worried in the face. I'll bet there were a lot of twisted-up thoughts wiggling around in his little head. Of course, when I saw him looking at me, I shut my eyes again quick.

"All right, Big Jim," Barry said, "let Poetry relieve you," meaning "Let Poetry take your place so you can rest." There was only a second before Poetry's big fat hands were pressing down with all his might, like a ton of soft bricks crushing the life out of me. I knew that if Poetry didn't bring me back to life nobody would—or else he'd be sure to kill me. "Ugh!" I grunted, "not so heavy!"

Then I heard a sound like more crackers being eaten. I opened my eyes, and there was Dr. Dragonfly with a forked stick for a doctor's stethoscope.

"He's breathing," Poetry said, puffing away with his own breath.

I took another quick peep through my thick red eyelashes and saw Dragonfly with his stethoscope leaning over me. Little Tom stooped down and stuck an open bottle of ammonia under my nose, which Circus had just given him, and which he'd brought with him, and which didn't smell very good.

"Put the hot water bottle here," Dr. Dragonfly said. "His heart is still beating, but very slowly." Somebody pushed a big flat rock, which was supposed to be a hot water bottle, up against my legs. And all the time Poetry was giving me artificial respiration, a new one every five seconds, which is fifteen times a minute. Or is it twelve?

"How is he, doctor?" Barry asked soberly.

"Another hour may bring him to life," Dragonfly said. "It sometimes takes *two* hours. Nobody ought to give up until they've tried for two hours. Unless there is a doctor there to tell you he is dead."

Another hour! Say! It seemed like they'd worked on me for three hours already. I opened my eyes a little again. I saw Little Jim sitting down under the willow with the little black-and-green turtle on his lap, not paying any attention to us. He had his knife out of his pocket. He was scratching away on the green roof of the turtle's house. *What in the world!* I thought.

Pretty soon, Dragonfly listened again to my heart. Then he stuck a feather in front of my nose and mouth to see if I was breathing and to see if the little fuzzy feather would move a little, which I was and which it did.

But Dragonfly was having a good time. He straightened up and said sadly, sounding just like a doctor saying something important, "The boy is dead. There's no use to continue."

Well, that was enough for me. I tell you I came to life pretty quick. I rolled over, shoved Poetry off into the water, and sat up, disgusted with everybody but very much alive.

Little Snow-in-the-Face looked at me and at all of us, and then grunted, "All white boys crazy." He started off on the run across the sand toward a little path in the forest which would take him back to his home.

I scrambled to my feet, covered with sand which stuck to my clothes because they were wet. I shook myself like a dog does when it comes out of the water and said, "I'm HUNGRY!" yelling the last word.

Just then Little Jim straightened up, scrambled to *his* feet, still holding the turtle. It's legs were sticking out from under his roof and were moving like Charlotte Ann's do when she's being held in somebody's arms and doesn't want to be, but wants to be put down.

I supposed of course that Little Jim was scratching his initials on the turtle's back, but he wasn't.

"Look!" he said to all of us, holding it up for us to see. And there on the turtle's bony back was printed:

JOHN 3:16

Which goes to show that that little fellow is always thinking the right kind of thoughts. "Let's take him back to camp," Dr. Dragonfly said, looking at the turtle, "and peform a surgical operation."

"Nothing doing," Little Jim objected. "Watch!"

Little Jim walked over to the lake. He stooped down and

65

set the little wriggling turtle in the sand right at the water's edge. Talk about anybody being in a hurry! You should have seen that little turtle beat it! In a flash he was gone, right into the water. All of his little legs were paddling fiercely, straight to the bottom of the lake, which was as clear as drinking water. And just that minute Little Jim said, quoting from the Bible: "Go ye into all the world and preach the gospel to every creature, baptizing them in the name of the Father and of the Son and of the Holy Ghost."

Some day, I thought, somebody may find that little turtle and read the writing on the roof of its house. He may look it up in the Bible and believe on Jesus Christ and get everlasting life, just like it says. Say, I wonder how many people in the world are as interested in spreading the gospel as that grand Little Jim guy of the Sugar Creek Gang? Not very many, I'll bet, or there wouldn't be so many boys in the world whose parents aren't like Little Jim's and mine, and some of the rest of the Sugar Creek Gang, Dragonfly's parents being the only ones who aren't Christians.

# 10

There were two surprises waiting for me when we got back to camp. The first was a letter from the folks at home. The other was what we found when we dug up our Indian dinner.

I think the rest of the gang was as hungry as I was. It took us only a little while to get back, not nearly as long as it took me to get there in the first place. As soon as I'd changed clothes, Big Jim said, "Bill, there was a letter for you. We left it in the box."

Dr. Dragonfly went along with me out to the end of the long dock to the mailbox. The dock was long because the water near the shore was very shallow, too shallow for a motorboat to run in.

Sure enough there was a letter from home, in my mom's handwriting. It told about different things, such as Mixy's kittens, blackberry pie for dinner that day, Big Bob Till's hoeing potatoes for my dad for two days and eating dinner at our house. Then Mom added some very unnecessary advice about me being sure to have good manners at the table, being courteous to everybody, and not to forget my New Testament. Imagine Mom being afraid I'd not have good manners away from home! I always had good manners when I was in other people's houses, or with other people. I was even beginning to have good manners at home.

Then there was a note from Charlotte Ann, who couldn't write by herself. She had scribbled and scratched with a pencil the way a baby does when her mother holds her hand for her.

Dear Big Brother Bill:
Mom and Dad and I had a three-cornered hug this morning, with Dad holding me in one arm and Mom in the other, and with me in between. Then Dad and Mom sat down with Mom holding me. Dad read a verse or two out of the Bible and talked about you and me. Then

he and Mom bowed their heads and shut their eyes and talked to Somebody about you and me and each other. I think I saw tears in Mom's eyes when they quit talking about us. Mom said to Dad, "I hope Bill remembers to wear his life preserver whenever he goes out in the boat up there." So maybe you'd better be sure to do it.

With love,
CHARLOTTE ANN

I finished reading the letter, feeling something like a big strawberry lodged in my throat. Thinking about the strawberry made me hungry. So Dr. Dragonfly and I went racing up the dock to camp, to where the gang was digging up the Indian dinner—the raw fish and potatoes and carrots and raw corn-on-the-cob, I thought.

But I thought wrong! First, they took off—Barry did—the sand and dirt, being careful not to dig too deep. Then he lifted off the rocks and the burlap sacks. And there underneath were the leaves, and inside that—Yum! Yum! I could smell that dinner ten feet away!

Barry set everything out on a homemade table in the shade of a big Balm of Gilead tree, or balsam, whichever you want to call it. Then each of us walked around cafeteria style and helped ourselves. But first, we all stood around the table, with the steam from the potatoes and fish making us so hungry we could hardly stand it. Barry started a little song which goes:

We thank Thee, Lord, for this, our food,
For life and health and every good. . . .

All of us joined in, even Tom Till whose voice wasn't even worth mentioning, 'cause it stayed on the same pitch all the way through. But Circus's high soprano switched off into a tenor that was beautiful and as clear as a dinner bell. We all had our hats off. I opened my eyes which I wasn't supposed to and saw Circus's brown curly hair looking like it had that night I told you about in *The Killer Bear*, when he went lickety-sizzle down the aisle of the big evangelistic tent in our

68

town—and his drinking dad got saved the same night.

Pretty soon we were sitting cross-legged, or squatting or half lying down in different places, eating the grandest dinner I ever had in my life. You should have seen the letter I wrote to the folks about it. I put what is called a "P.S." on the end of the letter and said,

> Dear Charlotte Ann:
> Sure, I'll remember to wear my life preserver. Think I want to drown in the lake when I have the grandest little baby sister in the world? With ears that look like halves of dried peaches glued onto the sides of her little round head that looks like a little pinkish-white pumpkin, and with dimples, and smiles? Tell Mom not to worry. Barry Boyland is letting me learn how to run a little outboard motor. Sometimes I go lickety-sizzle up and down the shore, when the water is not rough. But even when the water is quiet, we wear our life preservers. It's safer to have them on and we like to *feel* safe. Even if we did have an accident and suddenly found ourselves in the water, we wouldn't drown. We would float along, shoulders up, and be perfectly safe.
> So, little black-haired, rose-petal-lipped, grand little wriggler, don't worry about your freckle-faced big brother, Bill. I'll be seeing you in about ten days.

It certainly was great, though, running a motorboat all by myself. It was the easiest thing in the world to do. The directions telling how to run it were printed right on the top of the gasoline tank. Of course I made a few mistakes learning how. But after that, with Poetry and Dragonfly or some of the rest of the gang in the boat with me, I'd go lickety-sizzle out across the water.

The days flew along with plenty of fun and excitement nearly every day. We all learned a lot of important things from the Bible. There was a class every morning for half an hour, with Barry teaching us, or maybe Santa or Mrs. Santa.

We had fish to eat at least once a day, for once in our lives getting all the fish we wanted. The last week we planned to catch a lot of great big fish to take home, packed in ice, to show the folks that our fish stories were true. And all the time Poetry kept hoping he'd hook onto that big twenty-pounder he had lost that day. The rest of the gang hoped they'd catch it too, but none of them did.

Along about the end of the first week, a little stray kitten came into camp and meowed like it had lost its mother. Little Jim began to feed it fish and milk and different things, whatever it'd eat. It was called a tiger kitten, having stripes on it like a tiger has. It had the pleasantest face.

"I'll bet it's lost," Little Jim said in Little Jim's way of saying things like that. And right away I knew we'd have to have another member in the Sugar Creek Gang, at least until time to go back home. At first though, we could hardly walk anywhere for that kitten getting in the way and wanting to lean up against our legs.

"Do you know why it does that?" Little Jim asked me one day.

"Why it does what?" I asked.

And Little Jim said, "Why it leans up against your legs and pushes itself slowly past, then turns around and walks past your legs again, all the time kinda half leaning up against you."

"No," I said. "Why does it do it?"

" 'Cause," Little Jim said, grinning, "it likes to be petted so well. It can't wait for you to do it, so it *makes* you pet it. It makes it just as happy as if you were stroking it with your hand. Kittens have to have lots of love."

I looked at his big round eyes. And say, that little guy didn't even know he'd said something which my dad would say was very philosophical.

Before the second week was gone, Little Jim liked the kitten so well that we knew we'd never be able to go home without it. And yet who wanted any more cats around Sugar Creek? I also knew that Little Jim's parents wouldn't want another cat around the house. And the Collins family certainly didn't need any more.

It was still the first week, though, so I mustn't get ahead of the story. Pretty soon it was the first Sunday. All the gang dressed up in their Sunday clothes which they'd brought along, and we drove into town to church.

Talk about a church! This one was just like any ordinary one, except that about one-fourth of the worshipers were Indians.

The gang sat in a row by themselves. Santa sang a solo, which was the best I'd ever heard. Sitting right next to me was little Snow-in-the-Face, and on the other side of him was his big kinda fat Indian mother.

While Santa was singing, I looked for a minute at Circus. His eyes were shining. He'd never heard anybody who could sing so well and who was a real born-again Christian at the same time. And who was always trying to get somebody else to become one. Circus's fists were all doubled up, and he was almost trembling. I could see that he liked Santa almost as well as we all liked Barry Boyland and wanted to be the same kind of man they both were. After church, when Circus and I were standing out by the car watching the people go home, Circus looked at me and said, "When I get big, I'm going to be a pastor of a church in a big city, and sing and preach both." Then he climbed into the back seat of the car. He took out his knife, opened the blade, and looked at it like it was a very interesting knife, blinking his eyes a little like they had dust in them.

After dinner that day, we all changed clothes. In fact, we changed clothes first. And after we'd had a little nap, which is good for boys on Sunday afternoons, if you can get them to take it, we all hiked over to the railroad coach near the Indian reservation, to where Eagle Eye was conducting a Sunday school. On the way over we passed by the place where the neck of the forest is fastened onto its body. Poetry and I dropped behind the gang a little and planned an early morning fishing trip around the point. Our minds were all made up to catch that big fish.

"Look there!" Poetry said, pointing out across the lake with its big waves moving like lazy boys hoeing potatoes, not caring whether they moved at all. The whole lake, with the sun shining down on it, looked like a great big blue desert, with a gang of white sea gulls tumbling around up in the air above it. Poetry started to say:

O beautiful for spacious skies—

when we heard a twig snap behind us. It was Dr. Dragonfly. He'd heard what we'd been planning about the fishing trip early the next morning. "I'm going too," he announced without asking us if we wanted him.

"Nothing doing," Poetry said, shaking his head. "You're always sleepy in the morning. And we don't want you to fall out of the boat. Besides, we're going after northern pike, not walleyed pike."

Which Dragonfly didn't like very well, and which Poetry really shouldn't have said. Anyway Dragonfly's face turned red. He said, "All right then, smarties, I'll tell the whole gang right away!" He lifted his voice and shouted, "Hey, gang! Listen! Bill and—"

That was as far as Dragonfly got. We both grabbed him. I clasped my hand over his mouth. Poetry said, "Of course you can go, but for good sense's sake, *keep still!*" Poetry whispered the last two words.

The gang all stopped and looked back and yelled for us to hurry up or we'd be late to church. So we hurried, but the plan was a secret. And we knew that tomorrow morning the little outboard motor would be going out across the lake—that is, if we could borrow Eagle Eye's white boat, so we wouldn't be heard by any of the gang when we started out. The little motor weighed only fourteen pounds, so we could carry it easily without getting tired.

Boy, oh boy! Early tomorrow morning! It was great to think about! 'Cause already I'd rather run an outboard motor than anything, even better than I had liked to ride my bicycle when it was just new.

We hurried along behind the gang, hiking toward the strange new church. None of us had on our very best clothes, 'cause the Indians might not like that. They might think we were stuck up or something. Santa says that's the way people should dress when they go to help in a meeting in the city too.

Pretty soon we were there.

72

# 11

At half-past two that Sunday afternoon, we were all in the railroad coach church. There were a lot of Indians there, squaws and young bucks, which are unmarried men, and a lot of little papooses, which are little reddish-brown Indian babies about the size of Charlotte Ann. Nearly all the Indians had kinda sad faces. Not even one of them was dressed like Indians dress in storybooks. They were wearing different kinds of different-sized American clothes. The girls and boys had mischievous eyes though. I decided that when they were at home they'd be kinda like other children.

Big Jim and I sat together on one of the seats. Dragonfly and Little Tom Till were right across the aisle from us.

I won't take time to tell you all about it, but you ought to know that it was Little Jim who played for Circus's solo when he sang. It was great to look down the long aisle and up to the little platform at the end and see that little brown-haired pal of mine sitting down at the little upside-down suitcase, pedaling away. He played it like his very pretty mother does for our church back at Sugar Creek. Circus stood there behind the homemade wooden pulpit, lifted his head, and sang. He shook his head a little to emphasize his words, just like Santa had done in the morning. I don't know why I felt like I did, but all of a sudden I couldn't swallow. And a second later I couldn't see very well either. It was the same song I'd heard Circus sing before. I got to thinking about how his father had been a drunkard and had gotten bit by a black widow spider. And then one night he had been saved. And now Circus's whole family went to church. And maybe some day one of our Sugar Creek Gang was going to be very famous, and all the world would know about him. I made up my mind that I was going to be as great as Circus would be, only I didn't exactly want to be *great* either. I wanted to be—well, I wished I could be a very famous Christian doctor who would save people's lives. But that when people talked about me to each other, they wouldn't only say, "He's a great surgeon," but they'd say, "William Collins, M.D., is a famous Christian surgeon. He gives lots of money to help spread the gospel."

As soon as Circus's solo was finished, Eagle Eye stood up and had us all stand. Then he shut his eyes and prayed a kinda long prayer in Chippewa language. After that Barry gave a short sermon. And Santa and Mrs. Santa sang a duet which was grand, all about Jesus being "The Saviour for Me."

It was a kinda funny Sunday school. They kept everybody in one big class, and different ones talked to us. Pretty soon Santa had what is called a "testimony" meeting. He asked everybody that wanted to, to stand up, one at a time, right where they were, and tell in just about ten words, *where* and *when* Jesus had saved them.

Well, it didn't seem nearly as hard for me to stand up in that railroad coach and say ten words as I knew it would have been at home. Santa said he was saved in Long Beach, California, in a tabernacle which was built on a vacant lot on an old baseball field, on a spot that used to be first base on that ball field.

Barry said, "I was saved in the hospital a year ago. A Christian farmer from Sugar Creek came and talked to me." And again I couldn't see straight. The crazy old tears got all tangled with my eyes. Before I knew it I was on my feet, and saying, "Yes, and that Christian farmer was my father! And—and he's the best dad in the world. And I was saved up in our haymow one day while I was praying and reading my New Testament." The next thing I knew I was sitting down. And I guess I never was so happy in my life, which is the way a boy feels when he gets up like that in church.

One after another we stood up. Circus and Big Jim and Poetry each knew *when* and *where*. Then Little Jim stood up. He didn't say anything for a minute. Then he said, with his Little Jim voice: "I don't know any special place where I was when I let Jesus come into my heart. But I know He's there!"

Say! There were quite a number of people who had come out from town—white people—to attend that meeting. When Little Jim said that, two or three men with big voices up in

74

front of the church said, "Amen!"

Well, we'd all stood up but Dragonfly. I kept thinking about him and wondering what he'd do, of if he'd just keep still. But he stood up right after Little Jim. He said, "I got saved when I was sliding down out of a sycamore tree down along Sugar Creek, just like Zacchaeus did in the Bible."

That was all of us except little Tom Till, the new member of our gang. Pretty soon a big Indian squaw stood up and said something in Chippewa which I couldn't understand but which had the word *Jesus* in it. Eagle Eye's mom and his father stood up too, and even little Snow-in-the-Face. I was sitting right where I could look little Snow-in-the-Face in the face. I thought of all the interesting things I'd have to tell the folks when I got home.

All of a sudden, little Tom Till was standing, and gulping, and trying to talk, and couldn't. And then he did. This is what he said: "I—I don't know whether I'm s-saved or not. But I w-wish everybody in the world was, and especially my father and mother—"

His voice choked off and he sat down.

I forgot to tell you that Eagle Eye acted as interpreter. That is, he stood on the platform and said everything *we* said all over again in Indian language, just as soon as we had said it, so that everybody there would understand.

Well, when little Tom Till said he didn't know whether he was saved or not but that he wished everybody in the world was, Eagle Eye said that that was a good sign that maybe little Tom Till *was*. You know, there are a lot of people in the world who have opened their heart's door and invited Jesus to come in, and He has actually saved them. But they don't know the Bible well enough to *know* that having Jesus in the heart is the same as being saved.

Santa, who preached a short sermon right after that, explained it to us. He stopped after nearly every sentence for Eagle Eye to interpret for him.

It was a swell sermon, not very long. But it was the kind that made a boy feel like he wanted to be a fisherman like Peter and the other disciples in the Bible. They were always going fishing and having a lot of fun, but they became what is

75

called "soul winners" or fishers of *men* instead of just fishers of fish.

Say, while Santa was talking, I could almost see that beautiful big lake over there in Galilee with the pretty blue water dancing and sparkling in the sunlight. I could see the boats bobbing up and down on the water, with the big fish wriggling and bouncing around in them when they got pulled in. And then I could see Jesus standing over on the sandy shore where He had built a little fire that morning and was roasting fish for their breakfast. And I wondered if they knew about how to cook an Indian dinner, so they could let the fire go out and cook fish for two hours, and then when they were hungry, come back and eat.

Then I could see Peter, that great, big, rough fisherman, who made me think of Big John Till, little Tom's father, and maybe looked like him too. Only Peter became a grand Christian, and John Till was an unsaved man. Well, I could see Peter stop fishing all of a sudden, just like the Bible story says, and look over toward the shore to where the blue smoke was rising from the little yellow-tongued fire, with flames leaping up like Circus's father's hounds do. And Peter grabbed his fisher's coat, tied it on, and ran splashety-sizzle out across the shallow water toward the shore.

Then the rest of the disciple-fishermen came to shore in a boat. Only when they got there, there weren't any big flames and not much smoke, but just live coals, with fish broiling on them. That goes to show that Jesus knew all about how to cook fish the best way, over an open fire.

Well, it was a great story. After the sermon was finished, little Tom Till and I and a lot of Indian boys and girls were standing around the little folding organ near the platform. Different people were talking to each other and looking at Little Jim play, which he kept on doing. His playing was called a *postlude*, or something. Little Jim knew all about music and nearly all the musical terms—his mom, you know, being the best musician in all of Sugar Creek territory.

Pretty soon Santa walked over to Little Tom and stood in front of him. He reached out both of his big hands and put

76

them on Tom's shoulders and looked at him with his big, soft brown eyes. He asked him something which I couldn't hear. Say, little Tom Till dropped his head, and nodded it, and a couple of tears squeezed themselves out of his eyes and fell down on Santa's shining black shoes, like a couple of sparkling diamonds falling. And I'll bet if Jesus saw them fall, those two little salty tears must have looked more important to Him than a whole truckload of jewelry.

In a jiffy, big Santa's big arm was around little Tom. They walked toward a little curtained-off place at the end of the railroad coach. I knew that in about another minute there'd be another member of the Sugar Creek Gang who was born again—which is an expression the Bible uses for becoming a Christian. And you have to be that or you aren't saved yet, no matter how good you think you are, Old Man Paddler says.

On the way home, we were hiking back along the same way we'd come, with all of us walking together. Circus surprised us all by saying, "Guess what!"

We stopped walking for a minute. Circus was looking up at a balsam tree like he wished he didn't have on such good clothes, so he could climb it.

"What's so important?" Dragonfly wanted to know. And all of a sudden Circus forgot his clothes and went shinning up that tree to the first limb. He stopped and looked down at us, grinning like a half-grown chimpanzee. Then he said, "I've been invited to go to Chicago to sing in Santa's church, and over the radio."

I stared at him. Dragonfly picked up a stick and tossed it up at him. Big Jim's face was sober. Poetry started to quote a poem. He picked up a handful of leaves and tossed them up in the air and watched them blow away:

As dry leaves before the hurricane fly,
When they meet with an obstacle, mount to the sky,
So up to the house-top the coursers they flew,
With a sleigh full of toys, and St. Nicholas, too.

That verse is a part of the poem "The Night Before

Christmas," and St. Nicholas is another name for Santa Claus.

Little Jim said, "Why didn't Santa invite all of us to come?"

"Why?" Circus called down to us. "Because it's at Thanksgiving time. And there wouldn't be enough turkey for all of us and Poetry too. The turkey will be as big as a roast lamb."

"See if you can figure out this riddle," Poetry said, changing the subject:

> Two legs sat upon three legs
>    With one leg in his lap;
> In comes four legs
>    And runs away with one leg;
> Up jumps two legs,
>    Catches up three legs,
> Throws it after four legs,
>    And makes him bring back one leg.

As quick as Poetry had finished he said, "Give up?"

We finally gave up, and he explained it. "Man with two legs sits on three-legged stool with leg of lamb on his lap. Dog with four legs comes in, runs away with leg of lamb. Man with two legs jumps up, throws three-legged stool at dog, and makes him bring back the leg of lamb! Now hurry up, everybody, and let's get back to camp to supper." Which we did.

But it was an actual fact. Circus was invited to go to Chicago, with all expenses paid, to sing in Santa's big church, and also over the radio. Not only that, but he could ride to that big noisy city any way he wanted to, either on the train or on a bus, or if he wanted to, he could go by airplane!

Imagine that! By *airplane!* You can guess that I felt like Little Jim did. "Why didn't Santa invite us all to come?"

"Maybe he will," Circus said, just as we came within sight of the camp.

And maybe he will, who knows? If he does I'll write about it for you, and the Sugar Creek Gang will spend

Thanksgiving vacation in one of the largest cities in the world. We'll see the zoo and the museum and store buildings that are as big as mountains. Say, that would make a good title for a new story, wouldn't it—*The Sugar Creek Gang in Chicago* or *The Chicago Adventure.*

Pretty soon it would be night and time to go to bed. Early in the morning, Poetry and Dragonfly and I would be out on the lake fishing for a twenty-pound northern pike. Boy, oh boy!

Barry sent little Tom Till and me to gather wood for the campfire. Tom was very quiet while we picked up different-sized sticks. I knew he was remembering what had happened to him in the railroad coach church. All of a sudden he said, "My big brother Bob's been workin' for your dad this week, hoein' potatoes."

"I know it," I said. Then that little red-haired guy said, "Do you suppose your mom'll give him an extra large piece of blackberry pie?"

"Sure she will," I said, thinking about my mom's extra-kind face. And then little Tom Till said something that sounded just like something Little Jim would have thought of saying. He said, "I'll bet if your mom gives him an extra big piece of blackberry pie, and is especially nice to him, maybe he'll think Jesus is all right too. And it'll be easier to get him to go to church." I kinda felt when he said that, that he had said one of the most important things in the world.

Well, Little Tom and I came grunting back into camp with our big armloads of wood. Then he asked to borrow my binoculars, so he could look away out across the lake to an island in the middle, where the sun was shining on the tops of the trees, like somebody had taken a great, big paint brush and splotched a lot of yellowish-red paint on them.

"Sure," I said, "here they are," handing my binoculars to him. "Keep them as long as you like," which he did, not giving them back until the next day, which was the day of all the excitement in camp, the day of the big fishing trip.

# 12

That night around the campfire, just before going to bed, Barry gave us five Bible verses to memorize. I wrote them down in a little notebook, where I had a lot of other important things a Christian boy ought to know. One of the verses ended like this, "Follow me, and I will make you fishers of men." Even though I was remembering the sermon Santa'd preached in the afternoon, and even though I was actually listening to Barry's talk, I caught Poetry's eye across the fire. He winked at me, meaning, "Tomorrow morning early." And that reminds me, I forgot to tell you that right after the meeting in the railroad coach that afternoon, Poetry and Dragonfly and I had asked Eagle Eye if we could borrow his rowboat tomorrow morning early. He said we could and had handed us the key so we could unlock it.

So, when Poetry winked at me, my hand slid into one of my pockets. I brought out the key which I held kinda half hidden, yet so Poetry could see it. Dragonfly saw it too, but I looked at him with my eyebrows down so he wouldn't look happy and make the rest of the gang wonder what mischief was afoot.

We even arranged it that night so that the three of us could sleep in the same tent. Whichever one of us should awaken first in the morning was supposed to awaken the rest of us. I crawled into my sleeping bag and zipped up the zipper. I pulled the nice warm blankets close around my chin, 'cause the nights were always cold up there. And pretty soon I was a goner, which means I was asleep. I didn't know anything, only of course when a boy is asleep and doesn't know anything, he doesn't know it.

Right away, it seemed, I was awake again with something feeling like a kitten's feet jumping up and down on my stomach. I was terribly sleepy and didn't want to wake all the way up. But I supposed it was Poetry or Dragonfly, so I made myself open my eyes. Say, it wasn't even daylight yet inside the tent, although I could see out through a little crack where the tent flap was open toward the east. I could hear two people breathing, one on each side of me. So I knew Poetry and Dragonfly were still asleep. Yet something was bouncing around on my stomach, something that had little feet, and was using all of them.

You can guess I woke up in a hurry, sneaked my hand under my pillow for my flashlight, and turned it on, and—

Well, I stared at what I saw. It was a wild animal! An actual wild animal, a wild cat! No, not a *real wild cat*, but a wild polecat, which is a skunk! You could smell him. And anybody who knows what a skunk smells like, doesn't like it. That little black-and-white skunk stopped when I flashed the light on him. He just stared at the light, with his two green eyes looking like two tiny flashlights shining right in my face.

Before I knew it, I'd hissed, "SCAT!"

That woke Poetry up. He jumped like somebody had punched him in the ribs. He threw back his blankets and sat straight up, grabbing his nose quick with one hand.

Well, that scared the skunk. He whirled around like a flash with his big, bushy black-and-white tail straight up in the air, which meant he was angry or scared or excited and was going to spray his ridiculous perfume all over the tent. I'd seen skunks do that back along Sugar Creek when one of Circus's dad's big dogs was about to catch it.

"*Duck!*" I yelled to Poetry, which he did, and which I did even quicker.

Mr. Skunk, however, must have had good home training or else he wasn't excited enough. He ran like a kitten straight for the tent flap and went out, leaving enough of his unnecessary perfume behind him to make us want to get out too.

Dragonfly, as you already know, was always sleepy in the mornings. But all of a sudden he woke up, grabbed his nose, and said, "What on earth!"

Poetry shushed him, saying in a hoarse whisper, "We've just had company."

"Wh-what time is it?" Dragonfly asked.

I looked at my luminous-dialed watch. It was four-thirty. I stuck my head out through the tent flap and looked toward the northeast where the sun was supposed to rise. The sky was already a sort of pearlish pink. It was time to get up to go to catch that big, twenty-pound northern pike.

We dressed in whispers and crept out quietly, so as not to waken the gang in the other tent and in the trailer. We picked up the outboard motor and our fishing tackle and hurried away up the lake shore toward Eagle Eye's boat. At the edge of the woods we stopped.

We took stock: fishing tackle, live minnows for bait, which we'd kept in the live box at the end of the dock, and now had in a little minnow pail; the little fourteen-pound motor which Dragonfly was carrying by the rubber grip on its steering handle; a flexo-spout can of gasoline, 'cause the little motor ran out of gas about every hour. Yes, we had everything we needed. Our life preservers were already on and were tied good and tight.

A life preserver looks something like a brown picket fence, made into the shape of a vest, with armholes. Instead of buttons in front it has heavy, brown strings as thick as lamp wicks, which you tie. The "pickets" are kinda round-shaped and stuffed with something like kapoc and are waterproof. The whole thing is as light as a lot of goose feathers.

Pretty soon we were there. I climbed into the boat first, taking the motor with me. I went back to the stern and sat down and began to attach the motor onto the boat. While I was tightening the thumb screw button, Poetry unlocked the boat. Dragonfly arranged the tackle box and the minnows so we could each reach for an extra minnow without having to stretch too far.

In just about a jiffy we were ready. We shoved off and floated out until we were far enough for the motor to run without its propeller getting tangled up with the sandy bottom. Then I started the motor.

I felt proud to think I could do it all by myself. I was glad there wasn't anybody older there to tell me how to do it. I already *knew* how. When a boy knows how to do something, he almost gets mad inside when somebody older than he is starts to explain things and to tell him just *exactly* how to do it. Although you can't expect all the parents in the world to know that.

First, I opened the air-vent screw and the gasoline shut-off valve. Then I coiled the starter rope around the starting disc, moved the mixture lever over to number four on the dial, and did what I was supposed to to the carburetor float-pin.

There was already plenty of gasoline in the tank. So I was ready. Quick as a flash I pulled the starter rope. Just as quick the motor started, and we were off, puttuty-sizzle out into the lake. I made a few adjustments which I'd learned how to make. I throttled the motor down to what is called trolling speed, which is very slow, with the motor just barely running, and the boat just barely creeping over the water. Maybe old Northern was on this side of the neck today, I thought. The water was very quiet on this side.

I sat there with my left hand on the rubber grip on the steering handle, feeling important, feeling happy, and feeling like something was going to happen. Poetry had his line out in the water, letting it trail along behind the boat maybe about fifty feet behind and with a sinker heavy enough to keep the bait just as close to the bottom of the lake as possible without catching the weeds which grew on the bottom. I didn't even put *my* line in the water. I wanted to run the boat.

Dragonfly sat in the prow of the boat and kept his line out too, all of us feeling fine. The weather was just a little chilly like it is in the early morning up there. I steered along the shoreline, following the long neck of land down toward its point, staying about twenty or thirty feet out in the water from the bulrushes which grew near the shore. The water was *very* quiet. Every now and then we could see a splash in the edge of the weeds where a bass was probably getting his breakfast. In the east the big, round sun stuck its face up out from the earth, where it had been buried all night. It kinda wiggled its head up through a couple of reddish-pink clouds and started off on its day's work.

"Look!" Dragonfly said all of a sudden. Poetry and I

looked just in time to see a great big blue heron with wings as long as a boy start flying from the shore out across the lake.

I tell you I felt good. I also felt sorry for all the people in the world who ought to take a vacation and couldn't afford it. And I thought that all those people in the world who *could* afford a rest like the one we were having, and *didn't* take it, were just plumb crazy. Why, Santa says that even Jesus Himself told His disciples to "come ye apart and rest awhile." He Himself was always going out into the mountains or somewhere where He could be alone with the heavenly Father and get His soul rested. I made up my mind that when I grew up, I'd take my boys or let them go alone to some camp where there was real Bible training. I'd teach them to love the great, big out-of-doors, which God had made for us to enjoy.

I didn't have time to think long though, not much longer than it took that great big blue, awkward bird to gallop across the corner of the sky to another shore. For right that minute Dragonfly got what is called a strike, which means that a fish somewhere down in the lake was hungry and had made a head-first dive straight toward his hook and got caught. In a jiffy Dragonfly's eyes were wider open than ever. He was pulling in a fish.

It wasn't much of a fish, though. Just about fifteen inches long, a walleyed pike. He put it on the stringer without my even stopping the motor. We put-putted along with Poetry looking kinda sober.

"What do you bet I get my big northern?" he asked.

"You won't," I said. And just then something grabbed his line. His pole went down against the side of the boat with a whack, his reel started to sing fiercely, and Poetry's eyes looked like Dragonfly's had. *"I-I've g-got him!"* he stammered. And it looked like he had. Away back behind the boat there was a fierce boiling of the water. And up through the surface lunged a great, big snout with a body fastened to it as long as Poetry's leg—almost. It actually looked like it was as big as Little Jim.

The fight was on. All week Poetry had not only been watching Barry and others catch, but he had been reading up

84

on what to do in case he got one on *his* line. Any fisherman knows that if you try to pull a big fish right straight into the boat when you have a little pole and the line tests only about twenty-five pounds, the fish'll break your line like it was a spider web. And maybe break your pole too. You have to let big fish get tired out first.

So every time that great big, fierce fish started to run down toward the bottom of the lake, or in some direction or other, Poetry let his reel run with it. Then just the very second he got a chance, he'd start winding up the line again.

"Let him go! Let him go!" Dragonfly yelled, as excited as Poetry was.

*Zing*! Out went Poetry's line with the reel spinning like an automobile wheel in a race.

I shoved the steering handle over to the left so the boat would go around in a circle, just like I'd seen Barry do it. But say! All of a sudden old Northern decided he didn't like the water along the shore, and he started out into deeper water. Poetry's line was unwinding faster all the time, which meant that as soon as it had all unwound, the fish would snap the line and be gone.

I didn't even think, I don't think. But I opened the throttle and our boat leaped into the race with Poetry acting like an expert fisherman. He wound up his reel as fast as he could, with sweat running down his face and his breath acting like he was in a fierce foot race. Then, away up ahead of us, the water broke open and up shot old Northern. His big, long, ugly snout was about as long as a big dog's head. He stayed out of the water only as long as it took him to get back in again. But we got to see all of him. While he was up in the air he shook his vicious old head savagely like a dog shaking a rat, trying to shake the hook out of his mouth. But he couldn't. Then he disappeared, and Poetry's line went tight.

"He's gone to the bottom!" Poetry puffed.

I steered over in that direction, and it looked like Poetry was right. The monster had dived straight to the bottom of the lake and maybe had buried itself in the weeds. Poetry tugged on the line. But it was just like pulling on the line when the hook is fastened to a log.

85

"M-maybe he th-threw the hook out!" Dragonfly said, his teeth chattering like he was cold though he wasn't, but was only excited and scared.

Poetry grunted in disgust. He kept on winding in his line while I steered in a circle. We got closer and closer to the place where the line must have been fastened to the bottom of the lake.

I was beginning to notice too, that the waves were a lot higher than they had been. In fact, they were rocking our boat too much for comfort. I looked up. We were just even with the end of the point of land where the waves were blowing past. Before we could do anything about it, we were out in them. It had been quiet on our side of the point, because it had been protected from the wind. But out here the wind came across in a big sweep. The waves were rolling twice as high as our boat.

Well, there we were! I opened the throttle full force for a minute. But that little motor couldn't any more battle against those waves than a baby could against a wind storm. Yes, there we were! A great big northern pike on Poetry's line, and a fierce wind that we couldn't buck! Then like a sudden thunderclap scaring a boy, old Northern came to life down there in the lake and started running wild again, just as the boat began to toss around in almost every direction at once.

"Can't you guide the thing?" Poetry yelled at me. "Steer over there toward the sheltered place behind the point!"

"Steer nothing!" I yelled. "This little baby can't make it! It's too little!"

I caught a glimpse of Dragonfly in the prow of the boat. He was holding onto both sides with his knuckles white. But Poetry didn't seem to have any sense for anything but the fish. He didn't know we were getting into rough water. Or if he did, he was thinking about how hard it was to catch the fish.

Waves tossed up around like our boat was a little match stick and the motor wasn't any more than an electric fan. But would you believe it? Poetry had that old northern clear up to the boat in a little while. And that big fellow with his savage-looking eyes and teeth was acting tired. At the same time, I discovered how to keep the boat headed against the waves and not let it run in what is called the "trough." We were actually making headway back toward the point of land and quiet water, when Poetry leaned over too far and overbalanced the boat. It shipped water—a whole half a boatful in one big gulp, like it was thirsty and wanted to take in the whole lake.

Dragonfly screamed, and so did I. Poetry lunged back to the other side of the boat, just as Dragonfly and I did the same thing without even knowing it. The boat capsized, and all of us were out in the water.

# 13

In the water! With a hard wind blowing and beginning to blow harder like it often does in the morning just after sunrise! And with the waves getting higher, the farther out we drifted!

Barry had taught us all what to do in case a boat ever tipped over or filled up with water and we didn't happen to have on our life preservers. "Stay with the boat!" he had ordered in a loud voice, driving it into our heads like a carpenter hitting a nail hard to drive it into a piece of wood. "Stay with the boat! Don't try to swim to shore with your clothes on! Keep your body all the way under except for your head. Get to the boat and hold on! Even if it is filled with water, it won't sink unless you try to get in. Stay down low, and hold onto the boat, and let the wind blow you to some shore!"

Then Barry had told us to do the same thing if we were in a canoe and it turned over. "People who stay with the canoe and hold onto it never drown!" Barry said. "It's only those people who leave it and try to swim to shore who drown. Remember this! *Canoes never sink!* They do get over-balanced easily unless you keep your weight low in them. But they *never sink!*"

Well, we knew all those rules. But already we were a long way from the boat, which was right side up again but was, of course, full of water. Besides, we had on our life preservers.

I looked over to my right. There was Dragonfly struggling around, gulping and gasping, but his head was up above the water. I knew he couldn't drown unless he stuck his head under the water himself. His life preserver was holding him up. He was riding up and down, up and down, with the big, high waves, which had whitecaps on them and looked like a lot of live, mad snowdrifts.

Just that minute I had to think about myself. A big wave picked me up and threw me away over into the center of a low place, so that there were high waves on each side of me. About all I could see was the sky above me and high water on each side. I don't know how I happened to think of it but I did. I thought of the Bible story which tells about the time God's people came walking, or running, down to the Red Sea, over in Egypt. The angry Egyptians were behind them with war chariots and spears, ready to kill them. Then Moses lifted up a rod which he had in his hand and stretched it out over the sea. And the great big waves stood straight up on each side, so the people could walk right across the sea like they were walking through a long hall. My dad says that God did that for a very special purpose, and that He does the same thing for us today, only in a different way. When people have to wade through a lot of trouble, He makes the trouble stand up on each side so they can go through safely. And their souls will come out all right on the *other* side.

Old Man Paddler has gone through a lot of trouble like that, and he hasn't ever drowned yet.

Well, I'd had rides on what is called the *Tiltawhirl* at a county fair. And it had been lots of fun. I knew that if I could quit feeling scared, I'd have one of the longest, happiest, Tiltawhirl rides a boy could ever have, 'cause we couldn't drown as long as our heads were above water, which they were all the time.

I heard Poery holler just then. Looking behind me, I saw him. And say! That big, fat guy still had hold of his fishing pole, and the fish was still on the other end of that line!

The only thing was, if old Northern would decide he wanted to take a trip down to the bottom of the lake, and if the bottom happened to be farther down than the length of Poetry's line, Poetry'd either have to let go or else be pulled under. Or else his line would break.

It's a crazy feeling, being about a mile out in a lake, all wet from your shoulders down, and riding the waves, especially when the water feels pretty cold, although it was beginning to feel warmer all the time. I was glad there weren't any sharks there to eat us up.

Just then I heard a splash behind me. It was Dragonfly swimming toward me with a grin on his face. "It's what I kinda hoped would happen," he said, his teeth chattering again. "But I wish I wasn't so s-scared."

He reached out to grab hold of me, but I yelled for him not to. It would be safer for each one to be by himself.

"I want something to hold on to," he yelled back.

We'd have worked our way over to the boat, but it was drifting faster than we were, it looked like. There was nothing for us to do but what we were doing, which was nothing—only Poetry still held onto his fishing pole.

"I've still got him!" he puffed. He grinned at me like he was having the time of his life. "What you looking so scared ab—!" Poetry stopped when a big wave tossed him around and kinda splashed up into his face. But he was grinning again in a minute. "No use to be scared," he said. "See the island over there! We'll be there in about fifteen minutes, and then I'll land my fish."

Just the same I was glad we weren't adrift in any ocean or on a big lake that didn't have an island.

When a boy is pretty badly scared, he can't get over it right away either. So I kept on feeling funny around my heart and thinking a lot of tangled-up thoughts. It was a good thing Little Jim and I had had our strange ride on the hog house in Sugar Creek that spring, or our parents wouldn't have made us wear life preservers when we went out in the boat up here. I also thought that even if a lake *was* awfully deep, it wouldn't take a drowning boy long to get to the bottom.

We kept on drifting and calling out different things to each other, and beginning to feel almost cheerful when we saw ourselves getting near and nearer to the island. Poetry actually called out to me once, "Say, Bill! What direction are we floating?" Which made me think that on a map that was hanging on a wall, straight south was *straight down*! So I yelled back at him, just as a big wave came between him and me and we couldn't see each other. "If we hadn't put on our life preservers, we'd have all floated straight *south*."

Even though we still didn't feel safe, I knew we were. Yet my feelings and what I knew kept on arguing with each other, with my feelings getting the best of the argument most of the time. For a minute I thought of what Little Jim, the best Christian in our gang and maybe in the whole world, would say, if he was with us. I thought maybe he'd say something like this, "That goes to show that if a boy has Jesus for his Saviour, he is *saved*, whether he feels it all the time or not."

In another five or ten minutes though, we'd be to the island. And there maybe we could start a fire with a bow and a stick and some string, like Barry's been teaching us how to do. And we could send up smoke signals like Scouts do. And somebody would see them and come to our rescue. It'd be fun being marooned on an island.

"Hey! Look!" Dragonfly called to us. "The wind's going to blow us *past* the island!"

We looked, and Dragonfly was right. We were going to miss the island, unless—unless we could swim a little against those waves and keep from it. If we drifted past the island, we'd have to drift for a lot of miles before we'd ever get to land. The shore on the other side of it was a long way off.

Just then Poetry yelled, "This crazy old northern's got himself buried on the bottom of the lake and won't budge." Poetry was holding his pole up in the air. The reel was spinning around and around, as the waves washed him toward me.

"Jerk him!" I called back. "Make him mad! Then maybe he'll—"

Poetry jerked, and a minute later he was winding in his line again. That meant the fish was following along behind somewhere.

Just that minute also I heard a roaring which sounded like an airplane. I looked up but didn't see anything. I did see that we were going to miss the island, so I yelled to Poetry to let the fish go and to start to swim, or we'd have to stay in the water maybe all the rest of the morning.

But it was already too late. Dragonfly was already starting past, and I would be in a minute, and so would Poetry.

"Look!" Dragonfly cried. "Somebody's coming in a boat!"

Again Dragonfly was right. Straight toward us from away across the lake came a big, white boat that looked like

91

Santa's. A high-powered motor was carrying that boat roarety-sizzle toward the island and us!

"Hurrah!" I yelled. "We're saved!"

And we were! In the prow of the boat was little Tom Till, holding on tight with his life preserver on. Back in the stern were Barry and Big Jim, in Santa's great big boat.

I tell you it didn't take us long to get rescued after that. Dragonfly and I were in in a jiffy. Poetry was still holding onto his fishing pole. Just as quick as he was in, with his slopping wet clothes, he started working on old Northern. Within about three minutes, with a big gaff hook which Barry had in the boat, we had landed him.

Talk about a fish! Well, we never did quit talking about it, Poetry especially. It was a pretty wet, pretty scared, but kinda happy boatful of people that went back across those big, high waves, roarety-sizzle, toward camp. It was a tired and hungry three of us too, who after we'd changed clothes, sat down in the trailer in the dinette end and ate pancakes and bacon and grapefruit for breakfast.

"How'd you know where to find us?" I asked, kinda chopping off the last two words, when I bit off a nice juicy bit of pancake.

"Easy," Barry said. "Tom here was out looking at the lake with your binoculars when he saw you."

You can guess we were glad we'd invited little Tom Till to go along with us on our camping trip.

Maybe I ought to tell you that before we came back from the island we pulled that other boat up onto the shore there away from the waves. We took the little motor off, and brought it back with us. As soon as the lake should get quiet again, we'd go back to the island and get it. The little motor would have to have something done to it, of course. It was all water-soaked. I was glad it had stayed fastened onto the boat though, or it would have been lying down on the bottom of the lake somewhere like Barry says hundreds of motors are all over America, where somebody has been careless or has had an accident they couldn't help.

Well, I looked across the table at Dragonfly and Poetry. Then I looked down the length of the trailer at Big Jim and

Circus and Little Jim, who were sitting there on the daven-port, watching us eat and listening to us talk. And I was very glad to be alive. Everything was quiet for a minute. I could hear the drip, drip of water where the ice was slowly melting in the icebox.

Just then Little Jim turned around to where the mantel-type radio was sitting on the shelf behind him and turned it on. "It's time for the Children's Gospel Hour," he said, and in a minute there came fading in the voices of a whole lot of children singing a chorus we'd learned only a few nights before at our campfire:

> Broadcast the gospel everywhere,
>  Tell it to sinners far and near;
> Christ, God's Son upon Calvary's tree,
>  Paid the ransom for you and for me;
> Broadcast the gospel everywhere.

Between songs, I asked Circus, "Will you dedicate a song to us when you get to Chicago next Thanksgiving?"

"Sure," Circus said, grinning, "I'll even dedicate a piece of turkey to you when I eat it," which made Poetry frown and made me wish harder than ever that Santa would invite the whole gang to go along with Circus. I'd never had an airplane ride, and I'd never been in Chicago, or in a broad-casting studio.

Looking back over this big, long story, I see it's as long as it ought to be. So I'll have to skip all the things that hap-pened the second week of our camping trip. It was a great week, though, and we had the time of our lives.

93